D1359681

TALES FROM
BOMBAST'S BOOKSHELF

Also Available from Monkey Mind Tales®

Tales For Your Monkey's Mind
More Tales For Your Monkey's Mind

TALES FROM BOMBAST'S BOOKSHELF

STEVE MICHAEL REEDY

ILLUSTRATIONS BY TOM FEE

MONKEY MIND TALES®

Illustrations by: Tom Fee

"Monkey Mind Tales Title Font" by: Tom Fee & Steve Michael Reedy

Photographs by: Joanne Stegawski

Publishing consultant: Let's Write Books, Inc.

Disclaimer: This is a work of fiction. All of the characters, names, incidents,
organizations, and dialogue herein are either the products of the author's
imagination or are used fictionally.

ISBN: 978-0-9977920-4-1

Published by Monkey Mind Tales®
Dallas, Texas

Monkeymindtales.com
Contact@monkeymindtales.com

For My Family
(Past, present, & future)

I wish to personally thank the following people without whom this book could not have been created: Mike Reedy, my amazing dad (for his endless guidance, advice, and support), Judy Reedy, my mom and best friend (who took on the difficult task of editing my work to make each story the best it could be), my friends (who kept me sane), and all those who helped bring this book to life.

"A person who thinks all the time
has nothing to think about except thoughts.
So he loses touch with Reality,
and lives in a world of illusion.

Alan Watts

CONTENTS

LOOK OUT TOWARD THE SEA

Hey little monkey, climb down from your tree;
There's something coming in from the great big open sea.
It's built like a house. It bobs like a boat.
It looks quite odd, but stays afloat.
It's home to a couple who takes it on trips,
A man and his wife named Bombast and Pix.
Bombast is big, but he's gentle and kind.
Pix is as sweet as you ever might find.
They both never travel with fishnets and hooks.
Instead, they have shelves that are filled up with books.
Why don't we read one? Let's grab you a seat.
Sit yourself down and put up your feet.
Where to begin? Perhaps with a war?
Or secrets kept hidden behind a locked door?
A castle of candy? A creature that drools?
A mystery box? A tree that grows jewels?
This one is scary. This one is sweet.
This one has creatures with soft, furry feet.
How about this one? I think it will do.
It starts with a girl who was sick with the flu.

THE FLORALINS OF THE DANDALEEN FOREST

PAST THE MOUNTAINS, BEYOND A STREAM, grows the forest of Dandaleen. Through its leaves the sun shines bright, as does the moon in deepest night, lighting the ground from where there grows lilac, sage, and scarlet rose. Foxgloves, daisies, and bluebells too, enjoy the dawn and morning dew. Flying gently from each flower, through the trees and under bower, collecting oil in little bins, are the tiny Floralins.

What are Floralins? They are mystical creatures that live deep in the Dandaleen Forest, and they are never seen by humans. Any human living near the Dandaleen Forest knows they exist because of a lullaby that is sung to sick and ailing children, and it goes like this:

"In the forest of Dandaleen,
Beneath its canopy so green,
Far from sight, and past the glens,
Do live the tiny Floralins.
Though often sought, but never found,
They fly along the forest ground,
Healing animals hurt and sick,
Using flowers that they pick.
They often sing a happy song

And help the weak grow fit and strong.
May use a stem, perhaps a seed,
For those like you who are in need.
My little darling, don't you fret,
And don't you lose your hope just yet.
For I believe this song is true,
And I believe they'll visit you."

Young Clary had heard the Floralin Lullaby when she was four years old. She was the only daughter of a sheepherder and his wife, who lived in a small cottage, the back door of which looked out upon the edge of the Dandaleen Forest. She heard the lullaby during a harsh winter when she'd come down with a terrible fever. For three weeks her frail body was held in her mother's arms, with a cold rag placed on her forehead and the sound of the lullaby soothing her to sleep. One night, near death, just as her parents were about to lose hope, Clary's fever broke and she lived.

Over the next four years, Clary grew into a lively, happy girl with beautiful dreams that filled and fueled the limitless boundaries of her imagination. She never forgot the lullaby and always wondered if Floralins were flying through the forest just beyond her backdoor. She often went searching for them, but it wasn't until she was asleep in her bed and snug in a dream that a Floralin found her.

It happened one summer's night, when the air was heavy with the scent of flowers blowing across the glen from the depths of the Dandaleen Forest. Clary was sleeping soundly in her bed with her dog, named Dog, lying at her feet. As she slept, she drifted softly into a dream where her body lifted from her bed, floated through her window, and then flew into the cool night sky. She flew over a creek, through the trees, and then deep into the moonlit woods. Eventually, she came to a clearing that was covered with bright red flowers, which sparkled in the light of the moon. As Clary drew closer, she realized that the sparkles were coming from something flying above the flowers, several *somethings* to be exact. Clary thought they might be fireflies, until she saw tiny buckets held in the tiny hands of tiny creatures who were flying from one flower to the next.

"Floralins," she thought, as her feet touched the ground, though they looked different than they had in Clary's imagination. They were as tall as dandelions, as brown as acorns, and had twigs growing out from the top of their heads. Their wings sparkled as brightly as a star and hummed like a hummingbird. They paid no attention to Clary as they filled their buckets and flew back into the woods beyond the clearing. As each of them left, the clearing became darker, until only one Floralin remained. Instead of flying off into the woods like the others, the remaining Floralin flew across the clearing until it hovered a few inches in front of Clary's nose. Then it spoke to her.

"Whatever you do," said the Floralin, "don't open the box."

"What box?" Clary asked herself. Then she decided to ask the Floralin, but before she could, she woke up; and the forest, the flowers, and the Floralin were replaced by her room, her bed, and her dog named Dog.

Clary sat up. As she did, there came a loud *yawn* from the foot of the bed. It was Dog, who looked as if he had just woken from a dream of his own.

"I saw a Floralin," she told him. "It said something to me, but I can't remember what it was." She sighed, and then she looked at Dog more closely. "Your ears look bigger," she said to him, "and I think your nose is smaller."

This may have seemed an odd thing to say, but Dog was an odd dog—at least Clary *thought* Dog was a dog. A year before, Clary had found Dog lying in the forest with a wounded leg. She decided to bring him home and nurse him back to health. Afterward, he chose to stay with her and they became inseparable. But every morning when she woke up, she could swear that something about him had changed. One day his nose was longer, or his tail was shorter, or the color of his fur went from black to brown. He was quite an unusual dog and like no other dog in town. So, she decided to name the dog, "Dog," in order to remind her what he was.

On the morning after her dream, Clary and Dog ran out the back door and into the Dandaleen Forest searching for Floralins. This time Clary was searching for a particular Floralin, the one from her dream. *"If I find it,"* she thought, *"I can ask what it said."*

They searched all morning, and when the sun had risen high above the treetops, Clary decided to rest near the bank of a creek. She sat with her back against an old willow tree as Dog sat down beside her. She was tired from walking, and her eyelids grew heavy. As she began drifting off to sleep, she heard a family of birds singing in the tree above her. Her eyes drew open, and she saw something glittering beneath a tree on the other side of the creek.

"A Floralin!" she thought, and tried not to move for fear of frightening it. "Dog," she whispered to Dog, "don't move." Dog gave her a curious look, but did as she said, and watched as Clary got up and carefully stepped across the creek. As she drew closer, she was disappointed to find a tiny, black box instead of a Floralin. The box was tied with a black ribbon that glittered when struck by the sun. As she stared at the box, Dog walked over and decided to stare at it with her.

"What is it?" she asked Dog.

"I don't know," Dog seemed to say… without actually saying it.

"It looks like a present. Who would leave a present in the middle of the forest?"

Dog didn't answer. Instead he sniffed at the box and continued to stare at it with interest.

Clary thought for a moment. Then she said, "Maybe it was left by a Floralin." As she thought some more, she decided that the box must have been left by a Floralin—and that it must have been left for her. So, she picked up the box and sat down beneath the tree as Dog sat down beside her. She untied the glittery black ribbon, laid it on the ground, and removed the top of the box. She turned the box over, and a tiny glass vial fell into her hand, followed by a piece of parchment. She placed the box on the ground and held the vial up toward the sun. It seemed to be filled with some kind of black, slimy sludge.

"I don't understand," Clary said to Dog. "This doesn't look like a present." Then she looked at the piece of parchment and found that something was written on it. Though she was only eight, she was a good reader, but the words on the parchment were so small that she had to hold it close to her eyes as she read what it said to Dog.

"Congratulations, little one. The time for truth has finally come. Within this tiny box you'll find a way to open up your mind. You'll be alert. You'll be aware of things you never knew were there. Unlock your future's hidden door and see what life may have in store. Just bring the vial up to your lips, hold your nose, and count to six. Then drink it down; drink it fast, and you will see the world at last. A brand new life will then begin.

Congratulations, once again."

Clary looked up from the parchment and then down at Dog. "I think they want me to drink it."

Dog gave Clary a look that suggested he wasn't sure if she should. Clary ignored his look and continued to stare at the vial.

"Perhaps," she said, "if I drink this, then I'll be able to see the Floralins. Why else would they give it to me?" She put down the piece of parchment and decided to open the vial. The sludge inside smelled awful, and she understood why the note had said to hold her nose.

Dog began whimpering as she brought the vial up to her lips.

"Don't worry," she told him. "I'm sure it's fine. Why would they give it to me if it wasn't?" With this logic, she held her nose, counted to six, and then tipped the vial so that the sludge dripped onto the tip of her tongue. It tasted awful. She swallowed it, grimaced, and then waited.

As Clary wondered what would happen next—it happened. There was a tingling feeling in her stomach. It traveled up her back, along her spine, past her shoulders, and then it gathered into a ball at the top of her neck.

"*That's odd*," she thought, but before she could think anything else, the tingling burst into her head.

Clary let out a *shriek!*

The tingling deafened her ears. It blinded her eyes. It grew stronger and stronger until, with lightning speed, the tingling attacked her imagination.

Dog whimpered and whined as Clary stood up and tried to steady herself. She felt dizzy and dazed, but mostly confused. Then something even more horrible happened; Clary's imagination began imagining horrible things. They were awful, dreadful, terrible things, unlike anything she had imagined before. Within seconds, she found herself overwhelmed by every possible negative possibility her imagination could imagine—like losing her friends, getting a disease, or freezing to death from a drop in degrees. She might break her leg if she rode on a horse. Her parents might fight and then get a divorce. Her house might catch fire or get flooded by rain. Her clothes might get ruined by rips or a stain. She might trip on her feet and scrape both of her knees. Her dog might wind up with a circus of fleas. Her thoughts became darkened and filled with regret, full of foreboding and fainthearted fret. Her past seemed regretful; the present seemed grey. Her future looked dismal and filled with dismay. As all of these negative thoughts filled her head, she wished she were home hiding under her bed.

Clary decided that under her bed would be the best place for her to be, but she suddenly found herself unable to move, as if frozen to the spot where she stood. Every time she tried to take a step forward, her imagination imagined that whatever step she took would lead toward something horrible, or possibly something even worse than "horrible." So, Clary just stood there, imagining horrible things, until she felt something tugging at her. She looked down and saw that Dog had bitten into the lining of her dress and was pulling at it, as if he wanted her to follow him. Fearing that he might rip her dress and not knowing what else to do, Clary decided to follow Dog as he led her into a clearing somewhere in the middle of the forest. She was about to ask where they were, when she noticed that the clearing was filled with red flowers, like the ones from her dream.

Clary looked down at Dog and frowned. "Why'd you bring me here? We don't have time to look for Floralins. We need to go home and warn my parents about the stove … and the loose floorboards … and all the other dangerous things around our house."

Just as she was about to list what those "dangerous things" were, she became startled by a noise. At first, she imagined an animal had come to eat her. But when she looked down, she saw that the sound was coming from Dog, though it didn't sound like a sound that a dog would normally make. It was more like a whistle, mixed with a hum. Then Clary saw a tiny ball of light drift out from the forest and into the glen, until it hovered a few feet in front of them. As it rose from the ground and came up to her chin, Clary found herself staring at a Floralin.

Clary almost jumped with excitement, but decided against it for fear that she might sprain her ankle.

"Hello again," said the Floralin to Clary.

Clary was about to say "Hello" back, but was surprised when Dog said something instead.

"We need your help," said Dog.

The Floralin looked down at Dog and then back at Clary. "Your dog talks?" she asked.

Clary looked down at Dog, then back at the Floralin, and she suddenly realized what must be happening. "I'm dreaming," she said. "I must have fallen asleep under that willow tree."

"You're not dreaming," said Dog.

"And yet you're talking," said Clary. "I must be dreaming."

The Floralin landed on a rock a few feet away from Clary. "Your dog used our distress call. Animals use it when they're hurt. Are you hurt, child?"

"Not yet," said Clary. "But I might catch a cold, or fall down some stairs, or grow old and alone." Then she sighed. "I don't like this dream at all. I wish I'd wake up."

"She found some oil in a box," said Dog to the Floralin. "She drank it, and then she started thinking horrible things."

The Floralin frowned at the mention of the box. "I'm so sorry," she said to Clary. "I tried to warn you. The box you found and the oil you drank were left there by Doogle."

"What's a 'Doogle?'" asked Dog.

"Doogle is a Floralin like me," said the Floralin, "though he's no longer like me since he went to that tree." With that, the Floralin began to tell Clary and Dog the story of Doogle and of Doogle's unfortunate discovery.

It was a discovery Doogle had made while he was collecting oils in the forest near an old knowledge tree. Hidden in some brambles near the base of the tree, was an odd-looking plant with black, blooming flowers. Doogle had never seen such a plant before. So, thinking the plant must be a friend of the tree, and seeing no danger that he could foresee, Doogle decided to drink some of its oil. After he did, his mind became filled with thoughts that had never been thought by a Floralin. Everywhere he looked the world was filled with things to worry about, things he'd never thought to worry about before. Though overwhelmed with this worry, Doogle managed to make his way back to his village to warn everyone of each fear that had filled up his head. Luckily for the Floralins, without drinking the oil, such fears couldn't enter a Floralin's ears.

This made Doogle depressed, since no one could see what he saw. Because of this, he began spending most of his days in bed where he found it hard to sleep with all the negative thoughts in his head. And his negative thoughts created negative emotions, which made him feel even worse. The Floralins tried to help, but nothing they did seemed to work. All they could do was watch as Doogle's body turned grey from the skin to the bone and, as he got worse, his wings became hardened like stone.

One morning the Floralins found that Doogle had left their village with no word as to where he was going, but he did leave them a note that explained what he was planning to do. Doogle would return to the old knowledge tree, take the oil from the odd-looking plant, which the Floralins had come to know as the "worry-weed," and then give the oil to every child near the Dandaleen Forest. That way the children would see the world as Doogle did, so they could keep themselves safe from harm.

"And," said the Floralin, "Doogle started with you."

"Me?" asked Clary. "Why would he start with me?"

"Because he cares about you," said the Floralin. "He's cared about you ever since he healed you from that terrible fever you had. You see, Doogle's not bad; he just believes every thought his imagination thinks up. But the way that he thinks was poisoned by the "worry-weed." Then she rose up from the rock and hovered in front of Clary. "The worry-weed changed him, and now it's changed you. I wish there was a way I could help you, but we've tried everything: roots, leaves, oil, seeds…"

"Have you tried a *thought?*" asked Dog.

"A *thought?*" asked the Floralin.

"Yes," said Dog. "I have a thought that I use when I start to get worried. It always helps me. Maybe it would help Clary."

"It's worth a try," said the Floralin.

And so, try it they did. Dog sat beside Clary, who still believed she was dreaming, and he gave her his thought.

"It's like this," said Dog.

"A thought-thinking factory lies inside you,
Which imagines your world and defines what you view.
It builds you a future and past in your head;
You can *think* where you've been, and what lies ahead.
When fueled by wonder and run with delight,
Your past seems a marvel; your future seems bright.
When fueled by worry filled up to the brim,
Your past seems quite messy; your future seems dim.
The thing you must realize—none of it's real.
It's just an illusion that shapes how you feel,
A fantasy much like you'd read in a book,
A story that from which your mind can unhook.
To start, find the 'present.' It's what you can see,
Like flowers, and trees, and the birds flying free.
The wind blowing gently, ahead of the rain,
Worries not where it's been while crossing the plain.
If rabbits get startled, they'll scurry away,
But won't stay afraid for the rest of the day
Or fret about cold when it's sunny and hot.
Fall turns to winter, worry or not.
Squirrels gather nuts without losing their hair,
For worry is different than being aware.
Aware that it's fall, they store nuts in the ground.

If worried, they might store nuts all year round.
The mice make no monsters inside of their mind,
So under their bed are no monsters to find.
A fox won't regret when it takes a new path
And then falls in the mud—it just takes a bath.
So, when you are worried or racked with regret
And find that your thoughts are all filled up with fret,
Try purging those thoughts, and free up your mind,
By thinking this new thought to help it unwind."

And that was it. Dog had given Clary his thought. Then he stepped back beside the Floralin, and together they watched as Clary thought about the thought. At first it seemed to do nothing, but then nothing turned into something, followed by more somethings. The first "something" that happened was Clary's fists began to unclench. Then her slumped-over posture began to straighten. Soon her eyes started brightening, and a smile began to form where there had been a deep and troubling frown. It was a little smile at first, but as it grew, the dimples returned to her face and the color returned to her cheeks.

Dog began to wag his tail. "I think it's working."

Clary looked down at him as her smile grew wider. "It is working," she said. "It really is."

Yes, the thought had worked. The worry had left her mind, leaving her imagination free to create wonderful and beautiful things again. Overwhelmed with relief, she bent down and threw her arms around Dog, giving him the biggest hug she could give.

"At least now I can enjoy my dream," she said to Dog.

"But, this isn't a dream," said Dog.

"You're awake," said the Floralin.

"I can't be awake," said Clary. "My dog is talking. Dogs don't talk."

"Well," said Dog, "that's because I'm not a dog. I'm actually a Tegarwobble."

"What do you mean you're not a dog?" asked Clary. "What's a Tegarwobble?"

"We're kind of magical," said Dog. "We can change into almost anything we want, like foxes, birds, and things like that."

Clary thought about this for a moment. Dog not being a dog explained a lot. "I knew something was different about you," she said. "You never seemed to be the same dog I went to sleep with when I woke up."

"I'm only a few years old," said Dog. "I'm still learning."

"And you live with humans?" asked the Floralin. "I thought Tegarwobbles lived in trees."

"I did until I fell out of it," said Dog. "I turned into a dog just a moment before Clary found me. She nursed me back to health. After a while, I started enjoying being a dog, especially being her dog. So, I decided to stay a dog and stay with her."

"But," said Clary, "if I'm not dreaming, then that means Doogle is going to give that oil to every child who lives near the Dandaleen Forest." Then she thought for a moment and said, "Maybe I could give Doogle my new *thought*. It worked on me; maybe it would work on him."

The Floralin shook her head and said, "We think he lives several hills from here and that he plans on delivering the boxes tonight. You'll never make it in time."

"Only if she walks," said Dog. "You forget that I'm a Tegarwobble." Then, without another word, Dog began to change.

First, his legs grew taller. Then his back and neck grew longer, his nose grew thicker, and his feet turned into hooves. Within seconds, Dog had turned from a dog into a large pony, or at least something that resembled a pony.

"Wow," said Clary, with the sense of amazement that any child would have after watching a dog turn into a pony.

"This should do," said Dog, and then he lengthened his tail. "Like I said, 'I'm still learning,' but I'm sure I'll be safe enough for you to ride on. Now we can get there in half the time."

Clary squealed with excitement, clapped her hands together, and then hopped onto Dog's back.

Dog grunted a little, and then he looked down at the Floralin. "What's your name?" he asked her.

"It's Teek," said the Floralin.

"Well, Teek," said Dog, "you lead the way and we'll follow."

Moments later, Clary and Dog were following the trail of Teek's light across the clearing of wildflowers and into the forest beyond.

When the sun sat a quarter from sunset, Clary, Teek, and Dog reached the base of a hill and realized they must be getting close. They realized it because the hill was covered with warning signs sticking up from the ground, nailed to the trees, and some were even carved into the hillside. There was a sign that warned of falling rocks and a sign that warned to avoid the pox. There was a sign that warned of bears and bees, to bundle up when there's a freeze. There was a warning that warned of a poisonous frog, a warning for mud-slides, and a warning for fog. There were signs that read, "Slippery When Wet," "Get All Your Shots," "Consolidate Debt," "Beware Of Lightning," "Stay On The Path," "Watch Out For Floods," and

"Recheck Your Math." Each worry that Doogle had hoped to instill was warned by a warning he put on that hill.

As Clary, Dog, and Teek reached the top of the hill, they found a small clearing, which had an old oak tree growing in the center of it. The tree was covered in moss and a scattering of white mushrooms, the tops of which glistened in the shafts of sunlight. It was a peaceful, almost magical sight, except that every sharp edge was painted bright orange, and the mushrooms had signs near them that read something like, "Poison!" or "Don't Eat!"

"I think we're here," said Teek, who pointed toward a set of tiny steps that led toward a tiny door at the base of the tree. Then she landed on a tree limb next to Clary and Dog.

It was Clary who noticed the large pile of black boxes sitting behind the tree, each tied with a black ribbon that sparkled in the light of the sun. "Look," she said to Teek and Dog, "they're stacked almost as high as me." She climbed off Dog's back and then tried to count the boxes, but there were too many to count. "There's so many," she said. "He has enough for every child near the Dandaleen Forest… and other forests too."

Dog turned himself back from a pony to a dog, though a slightly different dog than the dog he was before. Then he took a step forward to get a closer look at the boxes but tripped over a piece of twine. The twine ran up the side of the tree and attached to a bell hanging over the tiny door. The bell rang, and moments later, the door was thrown open.

"Who's there?!" shouted Doogle from inside the tree. "Better yet, never mind. Just go away. You might have the flu, and I have no time for flus today."

"We don't have the flu," said Teek. "We're here to help you."

"Help?" Doogle *humphed* at the word. "I don't need any help, unless you want to disinfect the ground you're standing on before you leave. Now go away and take your germs with you." Then, without another word, he shut the door leaving Clary, Teek, and Dog staring at each other.

"That went well," said Dog.

"What do we do now?" asked Teek.

Clary thought for a moment. Then she reached down and tugged at the piece of twine. The bell rang and the door opened again.

"What?!" yelled Doogle from inside the tree. "I thought I told you to go away."

"We need to talk to you," said Clary.

Doogle was quiet for a moment. Then he stepped out from the shadows and into the sun. Clary shuddered at the sight of him. His skin was as grey as the greyest sky. His face and body were covered in lines, like the creases near an old man's eyes. He was hunched over, as if struggling under the weight of his wings, which looked as hard as stone.

"Why are you here?'" he asked her. His voice sounded more perplexed than angry. "You should be at home, warning your parents of all the things they should be worrying about."

"But I'm not worried anymore," said Clary.

"What?" asked Doogle. "You must be. You drank the oil. It's in your mind."

"Not anymore," said Clary. "It's gone."

"It's true," said Teek. "We found a cure."

"What are you talking about?" asked Doogle. "It doesn't need a cure. It *is* the cure!"

"No, it isn't," said Clary. "It hurts people."

"No, it doesn't," said Doogle. "You're spouting nonsense, and I won't stand for it." With that, he stormed back into the tree, but he didn't close the door this time. Instead, he came back out with a piece of parchment in his hand. "I'll be giving a copy of this to everyone who drinks the oil. After you hear it, you'll realize how foolish you're being." Then he held the parchment up to his face, cleared his throat, and read what it said to Clary, Teek, and Dog.

"Congratulations!

You've been cured of all your blindness. Now your eyes can see. So you should feel more frightened, not joyful, blessed, and free. The world is full of danger and things that cause you strife: conflict, harm, and hazards that could devastate your life. You need to feel uncertain, uneasy, and uptight. You need to be

more paranoid and sleepless through the night. You need to feel suspicious, more scared, and insecure—skeptically untrusting and nervously unsure. Life is quite confusing, so fill your mind with doubt. Be afraid of everything, and once a day freak out. You should never leave your house. The world has gone amuck. Stay in bed, or just play dead.

Sincerely, Me. Good luck."

As Doogle finished reading the letter, he tossed it through the door and proceeded to glare at Clary, Teek, and Dog. "The children need to be warned," he said to them. "And, I'm not going to let you stop me from warning them. Now go away before you cut yourself on something." With that, he turned around and prepared to storm back into his house.

As he did, Clary remembered what they brought with them and why they came all that way. Then she had an idea. "Excuse me," she said, just as he was about to shut his door. "I hate to tell you this, but I think that you've forgotten to put up a warning."

Doogle stopped, turned, and gave Clary a puzzled look, as did Teek and Dog.

"What are you talking about?" he asked her. "What warning?"

"Only the biggest warning ever," said Clary. "I can't believe you don't have a sign for it. It could ruin everything."

"What?" asked Doogle, now sounding panicked. "What warning?! Is it about the trees?" He looked up at the trees. "They could fall and flatten us. I've been meaning to make a sign for every tree in the forest."

"It's not the trees," said Clary. "It's much worse than falling trees."

"Is it that frog?" he asked. "I could swear I put one up about the frog."

"It's not the frog," said Clary. "It's much worse than frogs."

"Then what is it?!" he yelled. "What is it?!"

"It's a 'thought'," said Clary.

"A 'thought'?" he asked, confused. "What do you mean? You're not making any sense."

"It's a thought that could change everything," she said dramatically. "It could ruin your plans. It could tear down your signs."

"Not my signs!" he cried.

"Yes," said Clary, "and your guard rails, and take away your orange paint too."

"Not my orange paint!" he pleaded. "I was planning to paint the whole forest. The entire thing's full of danger."

"Well," said Clary, "if I tell you the thought, then you can make a warning for it. Would you like that?"

"Yes," said Doogle "Please tell me. Please."

"All right" said Clary, who then looked at Teek and Dog. They were both grinning at her, for they knew what she was about to do. Clary knelt down in front of Doogle, brought her lips close to his ear, and began to give him the thought that Dog had given to her. Doogle listened closely, making sure he heard every word. When Clary was finished, she stood up and took a step back beside Teek and Dog. The three of them waited and watched as Doogle thought about the thought. Then, all at once, he grabbed his head, started moaning, and began twirling around in a circle.

"What's happening?" asked Clary. "Did I say it wrong?"

"I don't think so," said Dog. "It sounded right to me. I think his old thoughts are just putting up a fight."

Dog was right. Doogle's old thoughts *were* putting up a fight, but the new thought fought back. Doogle shivered, he shook, and then he shuddered, as the worry in his head struggled and fought against the new thought. Then, all at once, a tiny light began to glow in the center of his chest. It started out as a glimmer, but then it began to spread and grow, becoming so bright that it made his entire body glow from the top of his head to the tip of each toe. The stone around Doogle's wings cracked and fell, as a flash of light, brighter than the sun, burst from his heart. His wings started to flutter and slowly began to lift him off the ground. His arms shot out wide, his head lifted toward the sky, and the light within him grew as bright as the brightest star. It was so bright that it seemed to fill the entire clearing and the forest beyond. Then, when the light began to fade, Doogle looked like his old self again, and he flew down to hover in front of Clary, Teek, and Dog.

"Are you okay?" asked Clary.

"I'm not sure," said Doogle. He looked dizzy and slightly confused. Then he looked ashamed as he saw all of the signs he had posted and the boxes he had stacked behind the tree. "I'm so sorry," he said to Clary. "I can't believe I did this. I never meant to hurt you. I never meant to hurt anyone. I thought I was helping."

"It's okay," said Clary. "If you hadn't given me that oil, then we wouldn't be here. And you wouldn't be *you* again."

"That's right," said Teek.

At hearing this, the smile returned to Doogle's face. "I am *me* again," he said, and he swooped into the air, leaving a trail of light behind him. Then he flew back and gave each of them a hug, except for Dog, who had walked over to the pile of boxes behind the tree.

"Now that you're *you* again," said Dog to Doogle, "what are we going to do with those boxes?"

"He's right," said Clary. "What if someone finds them?"

"We could burn them," said Dog.

"I don't think that would be a wise thing to do," said Doogle. "The ground's dry, and it might start a forest fire."

Dog gave Doogle a concerned look. "I think there might be some worry left in you," he said.

Doogle shook his head and smiled. "There's a difference between being worried and being careful."

They all agreed, and after some discussion, Teek and Doogle decided they would unwrap the boxes and take the oil to the top of the tallest mountain they could find. Then they would bury it in the deepest hole they could dig. Clary and Dog would have stayed to help, but they needed to get home by sunset. So, Dog turned back into a pony, at least something that resembled a pony, and Clary climbed onto his back. They both said farewell to Teek and Doogle, as Dog galloped off into the darkening forest. When they passed through the glen of red flowers, Clary bent down to ask Dog a question.

"Dog," she said, "now that I know you're a Tegarwobble, and not a dog, do you want me to call you something else?"

"I like 'Dog,'" said Dog. "And I like being a dog, especially your dog."

"I like you being my dog too," said Clary.

"Then you don't mind me being your dog when we get back?" asked Dog.

"Of course not," said Clary, "you can be my dog as long as you want." Then she thought for a moment and smiled. "And maybe every now and then, when no one's looking, we could take a ride through the woods together."

"Deal," said Dog, and then he galloped on through the forest with Clary on his back, chasing the sunset toward home.

And that night, as Clary slept tucked in her bed, there wasn't a worry inside of her head.

I hope you liked that story. Want to read some more? Here's one full of action; here's one filled with lore. This one has a boy who's setting traps beneath a tree. "Why?" you ask. Let's find out. Keep reading and you'll see.

SHINIES FOR THE PICKING LINE

BOTTOM TOWN WAS A TOWN WITH AN UNFORTUNATE NAME. At least, it was to a young boy named Zach, who wished he lived in a town called *Something* Ridge, or Lake, or Prairie. But the town wasn't near a ridge, lake, or prairie. Instead, it sat at the bottom of a steep, jagged mountain, and so the town was named Bottom Town. The steep, jagged mountain, under which the town sat, was named Mount Kerpuffin, though Zach never thought it looked much like a mountain. It looked more like a giant, upside-down thorn. It was wider at the top than at the bottom, which kept Zach—and everyone else in Bottom Town—from being able to climb it. Zach didn't know why the mountain looked the way it looked, and he didn't know why there was always a rainbow arched over the top of it both day and night. He thought it was truly an odd-looking sight, but the oddest thing about Mount Kerpuffin was how it got its name.

Zach knew that the reason Mount Kerpuffin wasn't named "Mount Jagged Spike," "Dangerous Peak," or "Treacherous Pike" was that it was named after the creatures that lived on top of it, the Kerpuffins. The Kerpuffins were tiny creatures, about as tall as a grown person's shin. They had short fur, long tails, and large eyes.

But, the most interesting thing about the Kerpuffins was that their clothes were completely covered in jewels, enough to make someone rich. And they called their jewels, "shinies."

When Zach asked his parents if anyone had ever caught a Kerpuffin, his mother gasped and said, "Oh no. If you catch one, it will scratch you. Then your ears will always twitch."

"So they're bad?" asked Zach.

"They're not bad," said his father, "just peculiar."

"Very peculiar," said his mom.

And they were peculiar. For, at the beginning of every season, the Kerpuffins did some very peculiar things. If it were spring, the Kerpuffins flew on enormous bats down to Bottom Town, where they left a basket of candy on everyone's doorstep. If it were winter, they left fruitcake. If summer, they left pie. If fall, they hid near gravestones and screamed at passersby.

At first, Zach thought his parents were the ones leaving candy, fruitcakes, and pies on their doorstep, but his parents always denied it. "The Kerpuffins are real," they would say to him. "They're as real as you or me," but Zach had trouble believing in things he couldn't see. So, Zach refused to believe in Kerpuffins.

That was until he was ten years old, when he was awakened on the first day of summer by a noise coming from outside his bedroom window. He sat up in bed and then looked outside, just in time to see a tiny creature flying away on the back of an enormous bat.

"A Kerpuffin!" Zach screamed. "They're real!"

"Of course they're real," said his mom at breakfast.

"You're lucky," said his father. "Not many people get to see a Kerpuffin."

Zach felt very lucky, and he hoped to see one again. So, for the next four years, at the beginning of each season, Zach sat by his bedroom window hoping to see another Kerpuffin. Eventually, he became discouraged and decided to stop looking, until the day his parents told him something that changed his mind.

It was just after Zach turned thirteen that his parents sat him down to tell him about the "Picking Line."

"What's a 'Picking Line?'" asked Zach.

"It's an event for boys a year older than you," said his mom.

His father nodded. "And it's held at the beginning of every season. You see, after a boy turns fourteen, he stands in a line with other boys his age or older."

"Why?" asked Zach.

"To get picked," said his father. "You stand in line and wait to get picked by a girl."

"For what?" asked Zach.

"To spend the rest of your life with," said his mom.

And that was when Zach learned about the Picking Line of Bottom Town, a tradition that sounded awful to him—not *awful* because he thought girls were awful—*awful* because he was afraid of not being picked. He heard the older boys say that girls liked "stuff," and that each boy was allowed to bring a pile of stuff to stand beside while standing in line. If a girl liked a boy's pile of stuff, then she was more likely to pick him over the other boys. If a boy wasn't picked, then he had to stand in the next Picking Line and try again. Some boys stood in line for years, and some never got picked.

"That's the worst part," an older boy told Zach. "If a girl never picks you, then you'll never be loved."

The more Zach heard about the Picking Line, the more worried he became. Living a life without being loved sounded horrible, but he needed a pile of stuff to help him get picked. His family was poor, and they earned very little. So, he had to think of a way to get a pile of stuff. He thought and he thought until an idea came to his head, an idea that involved a sign, a box, and a Kerpuffin.

— — — — .

The following fall a young Kerpuffin prepared to make his first trip down the mountain to Bottom Town. The Kerpuffin's name was Geo. He was a little afraid about the trip, but also excited, because he had never been to Bottom Town. He was a very curious Kerpuffin; some thought he was a little too curious. He had heard a lot about humans and was thrilled by the thought of seeing one.

To make sure Geo's first trip was a success, he was accompanied by a tutor named Old Jasper. As they both prepared to climb onto their bats, Old Jasper looked at Geo and grinned.

"Well," said Old Jasper, "you've got your bat and your hat. I'd say we're ready, wouldn't you?"

Geo looked over the edge of the mountain, then back at Old Jasper, and nodded his head a bit nervously.

"Don't worry," said Old Jasper. "It's autumn. All we have to do is fly down, hide behind some gravestones, and scare people… easy as that. At least it's not summer. There will be none of that flying-up-and-down-the-mountain, stacking-up-pies business tonight. The fruitcakes are worse. Nope, tonight should be simple; just follow me. You'll be fine." With that, Old Jasper climbed onto the back of his bat and nudged it gently with his feet. The bat lifted off the ground and hovered in front of Geo. Then Geo did the same with his bat, and soon they were joined by fifty other bats with fifty other Kerpuffins.

"The sun is down!" announced Old Jasper. "It's time to go!"

One by one the Kerpuffins swooped down the mountainside

toward Bottom Town. If the humans in Bottom Town had looked up, the sight may have looked like a black cloud had grown too heavy for the sky.

The Kerpuffins left their bats at the bottom of Mount Kerpuffin and made their way toward the Bottom Town graveyard. Once there, they each found a gravestone to hide behind. Old Jasper found two gravestones near a path that led toward town.

"This is a great spot," said Old Jasper. "We should scare a lot of humans tonight."

Geo knelt behind his gravestone and looked over toward Old Jasper. "Um," he said hesitantly, "I've always wondered… Why do we hide behind gravestones and scare humans?"

Old Jasper thought for a moment. "I'm not sure," he answered. "I guess because it's something we've always done. You know— tradition. Besides, the humans expect it. Some of them even leave us cookies."

Just then, two kids walked by. Old Jasper took in a deep breath and screamed at both of them. The kids screamed in return and ran as fast as they could.

"Just like that," said Old Jasper. "When they come, you scream."

Geo watched as the kids ran away screaming. "And, they like this?" he asked.

"Of course," said Old Jasper. "It gives them something to look forward to and talk about with the other humans."

Just then, an elderly woman approached them. As she did, Geo took in a deep breath, but let out a squeak instead of a scream.

The old woman looked toward the graveyard and sighed. "That wasn't very scary," she said. "Not scary at all." Then she walked away from them with a look of disappointment on her face.

"It's more from the chest," said Old Jasper. "Don't worry. You'll get it."

As they waited for the next human to walk by, Geo decided to ask Old Jasper another question. "I heard from the other Kerpuffins that humans are dangerous. I don't see how. They just run away."

"Oh, they *are* dangerous," said Old Jasper. "While some humans leave us cookies, others leave traps."

"Traps?" asked Geo.

"Yes, traps" said Old Jasper. "Traps to catch us, so they can steal our shinies."

"But why would they want our shinies?" asked Geo.

"I don't know," said Old Jasper. "I guess humans are attracted to shiny things. You know, like fish."

As Geo thought this over, a young couple walked toward them. Geo crouched down, took in a deep breath, and screamed as loud as he could. The couple screamed in return and ran away.

"Better," said Old Jasper. "Pretty soon you'll be making them faint."

They were quiet for a moment, until Geo thought of another question. "If they like taking our shinies, then why do we wear them? Seems it would be better to leave them at home."

"Leave them at home?" asked Old Jasper, who seemed shocked by the idea. "Kerpuffins are *nothing* without their shinies. Without them we'd look like a 'Gunny,' and we can't go out looking like Gunnys, right?"

"Right," said Geo, knowing that Gunnys were the worst kind of Kerpuffin a Kerpuffin could be. Gunnys had no shinies for clothes, and so they wore gunnysacks. No one liked them, or talked to them, which is why they always ended up living on the other side of the mountain. Geo definitely didn't want to be like one of them.

As the night wore on, the old woman from earlier walked passed them again. Geo took in a deep breath and screamed his loudest scream yet. The old woman screamed and then started laughing.

"Much better," she said. "I almost swallowed my teeth." Then she walked off, chuckling to herself as she went.

"You see," said Old Jasper, "they like it. But be warned, if a human ever catches you and takes your shinies, then you have to scratch the human. That way the human's ears will always twitch. It's like a punishment. If you don't scratch the human, then it might try to steal your shinies again."

"But," said Geo, "if my shinies get taken, do I become a Gunny?"

"Of course not," said Old Jasper. "But you have to scratch the human who took them. Only then will you get a new set of shinies. If you don't, then a Gunny you will be."

Geo felt a little relieved, but hoped to never get trapped by a human. He didn't like the idea of losing his shinies, and he definitely didn't want to become a Gunny.

After practicing with Old Jasper for two seasons, Geo was ready to try it himself. On the first day of spring, he flew down the mountain with the rest of the Kerpuffins to leave baskets full of candy on each doorstep they passed.

When Geo had only one basket left, he saw a wooden box with a sign next to it that read, "Look Inside." Curious, Geo landed his bat and decided to take a look inside the box. Once he was in the box, he found that he was the *only* thing in the box. "*It's a trap*," he thought, but before he could turn, before he could run, the lid closed and Geo was trapped. Panicked, he looked for a way out, but all he could find were some small holes near the top. Slowly he

peeked through the holes, expecting to see a dangerous and frightening-looking human. Instead, he saw Zach, who was looking at the box with the same amount of fear that Geo was feeling. Then Zach reached out and nudged the box with his hand.

"Hello," Zach said to the box.

Not knowing what to do, Geo said, "Hello," back.

"Um," said Zach, nervously, "I'm really sorry about this, but I... I need the jewels you have on your clothes."

Geo's eyes widened. "You mean my shinies?" he asked. "Why?"

"I need them for the Picking Line," said Zach.

"What's a Picking Line?" asked Geo.

"It's horrible," said Zach. "It happens four times a year, once every season. I'm fourteen now. I've been trying to catch one of you for the past year. I thought I'd never catch a Kerpuffin in time. My first Picking Line is only a day away."

"But, what is it?" asked Geo again. He was still afraid, but now he found himself curious. Sure, he was trapped, but he had never talked to a human before, and this particular human looked sad.

Zach *was* sad, and he sat down beside the box while explaining why. He told Geo about the Picking Line, of being poor, and of his fear of not being picked. As Geo listened, he began to feel sorry for Zach. Geo thought Zach seemed like a nice enough human, even if he had trapped him in a box.

"I'll only get picked if I bring a pile of stuff," said Zach. "But, I don't have any stuff to bring. If I had your jewels, then I could buy some stuff; and if I have enough stuff, then I might get picked."

Geo thought the Picking Line sounded awful, and the more he heard, the more he felt bad for Zach. He hated to see someone so unhappy, so he decided to help. "No need to cry," said Geo. "Let me out of this box, and I'll give you my shinies."

"Really?" asked Zach. "You mean it? This isn't a trick?"

"I mean it," said Geo. "No trick."

With some hesitation, Zach reached down and opened the box. Then he stepped away as Geo climbed out of it. Geo, who was happy to be out of the box, took off his shinies and gave them to Zach.

"Thank you," said Zach. "Now I'm sure to get picked." Then he looked down at Geo and smiled. "I'm Zach," he said.

"I'm Geo," said Geo, who smiled back. But as he did, he remembered what Old Jasper had told him: *You have to scratch the human. Only then will you get a new set of shinies.*" Geo knew, if he scratched Zach, it would make Zach miserable for the rest of his life. How would that help him? It wouldn't. So, Geo decided not to scratch Zach, and winked at him instead. Then, without his shinies, Geo returned to his bat and flew up the side of Mount Kerpuffin. As he did, Zach rushed off to buy a pile of stuff for the Picking Line.

Back at the village under the rainbow, Geo was met by Old Jasper and the other Kerpuffins who looked at him in shock.

"Where are your shinies?" asked Old Jasper.

Geo stared at them, as they stared at him, and wondered what he should say. He knew that if he told them the truth they would turn him into a Gunny, so he thought of a story to tell them instead. It was a good story, one of dangerous peril, a desperate escape, and a mob that he had to outrun. This left Old Jasper and the rest of the Kerpuffins in awe of what he had done.

"But," asked Old Jasper, "did you scratch the one who took them?"

"Um, yes," said Geo. "Yes, I did." He had never told a lie before, but he guessed he told it well since they agreed to replace his shinies.

"You were very brave," said Old Jasper, "but be more careful next time. Remember, Kerpuffins are *nothing* without their shinies."

"I'll be more careful," said Geo. "I promise."

"Good," said Old Jasper. "Now," he said to the other Kerpuffins, "let's prepare for summer."

The following day in Bottom Town, every boy who was Zach's age or older, and had yet to be picked by a girl, made his way to the middle of town to stand in the Picking Line—each with a pile of stuff. As a girl walked by, she would look at the boy, look at his stuff, and then decide if that was the boy she wanted to pick.

Zach stood in line with his pile of stuff, as girl after girl walked up to him and then walked away. This continued for the rest of the day until one girl stopped, looked at his pile of stuff, and sighed.

"What is it?" asked Zach, wondering why the girl was sighing.

"Well," said the girl, "I like what you've got, but it's just not enough. For me to pick you, I will need some more stuff."

"Like what?" asked Zach.

"Well," said the girl, "I have lots of fears. I'm told quite a few, like spiders, lightening, and catching a flu—plus lizards, squirrels, snails without shells, blizzards, burrows, badgers, and bells. But fear of the future, and what it might bring, is why I am looking to wear someone's ring. I need to feel stable. I need to feel set, and the needs that I'm needing must always be met. The person I pick must be loaded and rich. I don't want to wind up dirt poor in a ditch. I don't have to love him; I just want his wealth. I need it to balance my own mental health. I might seem unfeeling, perhaps even cold, but all of my fears can be settled with gold. My love is conditioned, and so you must give all that I'll need for as long as you live."

Before Zach could think of something to say, the girl decided to pick a different boy with a bigger pile of stuff. Rejected, he waited for another girl, but another girl never came. By the end of the day, Zach had not been picked. The reason, he guessed, was that he needed more stuff. So, he went home and came up with a plan, a plan that involved a potted flower, a net, and a Kerpuffin.

The Kerpuffins spent that spring making pies for the humans in Bottom Town. They gave Geo a new set of shinies, picked from the forest of "gem trees" that grew at the top of Mount Kerpuffin. Unlike regular trees that grew fruit or nuts, gem trees grew jewels. The jewels they grew were so bright that they created the rainbow that hung above the Kerpuffins' village.

As Geo made his pies for summer, he often thought about Zach and wondered if he had been picked. Geo also wondered why humans judged each other based on the amount of stuff they had. It seemed silly to him. Then again, humans did silly things.

On the first day of summer, Geo and the rest of the Kerpuffins brought their pies down from the top of Mount Kerpuffin and left them on each doorstep they passed. As Geo was about to leave a pie on someone's doorstep, he saw a potted flower. It was a beautiful flower, and there was a sign next to it that read, "Smell Me." Curious, Geo landed his bat and went to smell the flower. As he was about to take a sniff, he heard a noise and looked up just in time to see a net falling from the sky. He gasped and tried to run, but his feet were too slow. A second later he found himself trapped—again.

"Geo?" asked Zach, as he walked up to the net.

Geo managed to turn over and saw Zach staring at him through the net. "Zach, why are you trapping me again?"

"I'm sorry," said Zach, "but I need the jewels from your clothes."

"What? Why?" asked Geo. "I already gave them to you once."

"I know," said Zach, "but they weren't enough. I didn't get picked." Then he sat down beside Geo and told him the story of what happened. When he finished, he said, "That's why I need more jewels. I need more stuff. If I have more stuff, then whoever picks me can feel safe and secure. The next Picking Line is only a few days away, and I just have to get picked this time."

Geo could hear the hurt in Zach's voice. He guessed it must feel awful not to get picked, and so he decided to give Zach his shinies. Zach thanked him over and over again as he helped Geo out of the net.

"Wow," said Zach, when Geo handed him the shinies. "Now I'm sure to get picked."

For the second time, Geo left without scratching Zach. Instead, he wished Zach good luck and flew back up the side of Mount Kerpuffin. As he did, Zach rushed off to buy a bigger pile of stuff for the Picking Line.

Back at the village under the rainbow, Geo told Old Jasper and the rest of the Kerpuffins a bigger lie than the one before. The Kerpuffins stared at Geo in awe as he told his story, while gasping in fear with every detail.

"But," asked Old Jasper, "did you scratch the one who took them?"

"Yes," answered Geo, "I did." This was the second lie he had told, and he hoped not to tell any more. He didn't like lying, but guessed his lie worked because they gave him more shinies than they gave him before.

"But remember," said Old Jasper, "Kerpuffins are *nothing* without their shinies. Don't get trapped again."

"I won't," said Geo. "I promise."

"Okay then," said Old Jasper, "let's start practicing our screams. Autumn will be here soon, and the humans in Bottom Town are expecting to be frightened."

During the next Picking Line, Zach stood beside a much larger pile of stuff. He stood there all day waiting for a girl to approach him, but none of them did. As the day neared its end, he almost lost hope, but then a girl stopped in front of him. She looked at him, looked at his stuff, and then shook her head.

"What's wrong?" asked Zach, wondering why the girl was shaking her head.

"Humm," said the girl, "I like what you've got, but it's just not enough. For me to pick you, I will need some more stuff."

"Like what?" asked Zach. "I have twice as much stuff as I did last time.

"Well," said the girl, "I'm insecure and have low self-esteem. My need for approval is somewhat extreme. I think lots of things that aren't always true, which sit in my head where they simmer and stew—creating suspicions and issues with trust, plus negative feelings that make me combust. I have a disorder, but gifts are the cure. They sooth all my worries and make me feel sure that the giver *must* love me—he won't plan to stray—and I can feel happy, at least for that day. My love will be his if I'm gifted with things. My favorites are chocolates, cute dresses, and rings—plus puppies, gold pendants, and shoes with a heel. The more that I'm gifted the better I feel. My self-worth is fragile, I have to admit. Just gift me with things, and we'll make a good fit."

Zach stared at the girl as she stared at his pile of stuff, but then she saw another boy with a bigger pile of stuff and decided to pick him instead.

By the end of the day, Zach was not picked. He figured he just needed more stuff. So, that night he came up with a plan, a plan that involved a shovel, a pillow, and a Kerpuffin.

As the Kerpuffins spent the summer practicing their screams, Geo wondered if Zach had been picked. He also wondered why stuff made humans feel safe and secure. It seemed silly to him. Then again, humans were silly creatures.

That autumn, Geo and the rest of the Kerpuffins flew down from the top of Mount Kerpuffin to scare humans. As Geo set out to find a gravestone, he came across one with a pillow in front of it.

"*That would be a perfect place to sit tonight,*" he thought. So he walked over to the pillow and sat down. Then, not a second after he sat, the ground beneath him caved in, and Geo fell into a hole.

"Hello," said Zach, who was now standing above the hole.

"Zach!" Geo screamed, "Get me out of here! I fell in someone's grave!"

"No, you didn't," said Zach. "It's not a grave. I dug the hole."

"What?" asked Geo. "Why would you do that?"

"Because I need more jewels," said Zach.

Geo stopped panicking as he realized he was not in a grave. He was in another trap. "But why?" he asked. "I've already given them to you twice."

"I know," said Zach, "but no one picked me again. It was awful." Then he told Geo the story of what happened to him at the Picking Line. "And that's why I need more jewels," he said. "I need more stuff. If I have more stuff, then I'll look trustworthy, and I can use it to prove my love to the girl who picks me. The next Picking Line is coming up and someone has to pick me this time."

As Geo listened, he could hear the hurt in Zach's voice. Then he looked down at his shinies. He had more shinies than ever before, and he thought they would surely be enough to help Zach get picked. Then Zach could be happy again.

"Okay," said Geo, finally, "I'll give them to you."

"Oh, thank you," said Zach, as he helped Geo out of the hole.

Geo brushed himself off and then handed his shinies to Zach. "I hope you get picked this time," he said.

Zach groaned, while nodding his head. "So do I," he said. "It's dreadful standing in line waiting to get picked."

Geo could tell by the look in Zach's eyes that it must have

been. So, for the third time, Geo left without scratching Zach and flew back up the side of Mount Kerpuffin. As he did, Zach rushed off to buy an even bigger pile of stuff for the Picking Line.

Back at the village under the rainbow, Old Jasper and the rest of the Kerpuffins were shocked to find that Geo had been trapped again.

"How?" asked Old Jasper, who sounded more angry than concerned this time. "How could this happen? No one has ever been trapped in the fall, no one! You just sit behind something and scream. That's it!"

"I know," said Geo. Old Jasper had never spoken to him like that, and the rest of the Kerpuffins looked just as angry. He gave them a story, and it was his best story yet, but no one seemed impressed.

After a long silence, Old Jasper shook his head and stared at Geo. "Did you scratch the human who took them?" he asked, with suspicion in his voice.

"Yes," answered Geo, quickly. "I did." But he didn't think Old Jasper believed him, and neither did the others by the look of them.

"Okay," said Old Jasper, flatly. "I guess it's possible." Then he stared at Geo for a moment… grunted, turned, and walked away.

The other Kerpuffins followed Old Jasper, leaving Geo standing alone on the side of the mountain. As the bats returned to their caves, Geo lowered his head and sighed. "I wonder if he believes me," he said to himself. "I wonder if any of them believe me."

During the next Picking Line, Zach stood next to an even bigger pile of stuff. But not a single girl looked his way. By the end of the day, Zach couldn't take it anymore. "Hey," he said to one of the girls. "Why don't you pick me? I've got *lots* of stuff."

The girl looked at him, looked at his stuff, and frowned.

"Why are you frowning?" he asked. He was sure he had enough stuff this time, but he was wrong.

"Well," said the girl, "I like what you've got, but it's just not enough. For me to pick you, I will need some more stuff."

"More than this?" asked Zach, pointing to his now extremely large pile of stuff.

The girl nodded. "You see," she said, "the path for my life has already been laid. It's filled up with milestones that can't be delayed. Right now, I'm behind; I need someone new. I married three others, but they didn't do. I'll stay on my schedule if you play your part— look dignified, doating, affluent, and smart. The man who you are doesn't matter to me. You must be the man that I want you to be. You'll also provide all the needs that I'll need: a homestead, a wagon, and kids that you'll feed—plus anything else that will help me look good. Our life must seem perfect. Is that understood? The more you provide me, the less I'll complain. Just stick to my plan, or I might go insane. Be pliable, moldable, dutiful too, and I won't reject you for somebody new."

Zach's mouth dropped open. As it did, the girl noticed a boy with a bigger pile of stuff, and she decided to pick him instead. Zach couldn't believe it. He felt awful, and as he walked home, he figured that the only way he was sure to get picked was to have a bigger pile of stuff, bigger than anyone else's pile of stuff. So, that night he came up with a plan, a plan that involved a chair, a bucket, a rope, and a Kerpuffin.

As the Kerpuffins spent the fall making fruitcakes for the humans in Bottom Town, Geo wondered if Zach had been picked. He hoped so, because he wasn't sure Old Jasper and the other Kerpuffins would believe another story. He also wondered how stuff could make humans look trustworthy or help them prove their love. It seemed silly to him, though humans were proving to be sillier than he had thought them to be.

On the first day of winter, Geo and the rest of the Kerpuffins prepared to deliver their fruitcakes. As Geo was about to get on his bat, he felt a hand on his shoulder.

"I need to talk to you," said a voice from behind him.

Geo turned around to find Old Jasper with a look on his face that suggested Geo was in trouble, and he was.

"Geo," he said sternly, "remove your shinies."

"What?" asked Geo. "You want my shinies?"

"Yes," said Old Jasper. "We don't think you understand how important they are. Therefore, we've decided you must live like a Gunny until you do."

Geo's eyes widened as his heart sank. "Will I get them back?" he asked.

Old Jasper frowned. "Not until you've learned your lesson," he said. With that, he took Geo's shinies and handed him a gunnysack. "Now," he said, as he walked away, "go deliver your fruitcakes."

Feeling embarrassed and sad, Geo put on the gunnysack. It itched him. He scratched at it for a moment. Then he climbed onto the back of his bat and flew down the mountainside, while fighting his tears as he went.

As Geo delivered his fruitcakes, he came across a comfortable chair. It didn't look especially comfortable to him, but it had a sign proclaiming that it was the most comfortable chair in Bottom Town. Curious and tired, Geo landed his bat and decided to see how comfortable the most comfortable chair could be. The chair was much taller than he was, so he bent his knees and jumped as high

as he could. It took three tries, but he was finally able to land on the seat. Just as he did, the fabric tore beneath the weight of him. A moment later he found himself being lifted out of the chair in a bucket. The bucket was attached to a rope, which was hanging from a tree. Geo looked over the top of the bucket and saw Zach pulling on the rope. Then Zach tied the rope to the tree, leaving Geo hanging seven feet above the ground.

"Zach!" Geo yelled down to Zach. "Why are you trapping me again?"

"I'm sorry, Geo," said Zach. "I didn't want to, but I didn't get picked again." Then Zach told Geo the story of what happened at the Picking Line. "And that's why I need more jewels," he said. "I figure the only way I'm going to get picked is if I have a pile of stuff that's bigger than anyone else's pile of stuff. Then a girl will have to pick me. I'll be able to give her whatever she needs, and be whoever she wants. I just have to…"

"Zach," said Geo, interrupting him. "I'm sorry. I really am, but I can't help you this time."

"What?" asked Zach. "Why?" A look of desperation fell across his face. "You have to," he pleaded. "If you don't, I won't get picked." Then Zach sounded panicked. "I'll wind up alone with no one to love. You just have to help me. I don't want to stand in the Picking Line anymore. It's awful. I just need more stuff."

"Even if I wanted to help you, I can't," said Geo, his voice quivering. "They took away my shinies. They took them away, Zach, and I don't know if I'll ever get them back." Then Geo started crying. "Kerpuffins are *nothing* without their shinies, and now I'm *nothing*."

Zach lowered the bucket so that Geo could climb out of it. Geo wiped the tears from his eyes and sat down next to his bat.

"Why did they take them?" asked Zach, as he sat down beside Geo.

"Because I kept giving them to you," said Geo. "We have a rule. If a human takes our shinies, then we're supposed to scratch it. If we scratch it, then its ears will always twitch, and it will never do it again."

"But," said Zach, confused, "you didn't scratch me."

"No," said Geo, "I wanted you to be happy."

The expression on Zach's face changed as he realized what Geo had done for him. Not knowing what to say, he reached over to pat Geo on the back, but pulled his hand away when it touched

Geo's gunnysack. "What are you wearing?" asked Zach. "It feels scratchy."

"It is," said Geo. "It's what we have to wear when we don't have shinies... and they call us Gunnys... and no one likes Gunnys."

"That's awful," said Zach. "I'm sorry. I didn't know."

"It's okay," said Geo. Then he stood up and handed Zach a fruitcake. "It was my decision," he said. "But, now I have to go back and face everyone."

Before Zach could say anything else, Geo wished him good luck, returned to his bat, and flew up the side of Mount Kerpuffin.

Back at the village under the rainbow, Geo didn't tell anyone that he had been trapped again, not that anyone asked. Old Jasper and the rest of the Kerpuffins ignored him. They continued ignoring him through the winter, as they prepared baskets of candy to give out in the spring. Geo tried to talk to some of the Kerpuffins, but they just looked away and said nothing. This left him feeling lonely and sad. Some nights he lay on the ground while looking up at the rainbow and thinking about Zach. He wondered why Zach would want to be someone he wasn't, just to get picked. It seemed silly to Geo, but the more rejected he felt, the less silly it seemed.

On the first day of spring, Geo and the rest of the Kerpuffins prepared to deliver baskets of candy to the humans in Bottom Town. As Geo loaded up his bat, he saw Old Jasper and asked if he could have his shinies back. Old Jasper said nothing. Instead, he climbed onto the back of his bat and flew down the mountain with the rest of the Kerpuffins, leaving Geo standing there alone on the edge of the cliff. Feeling sad, he scratched at his gunnysack, then he climbed onto the back of his bat and flew down the mountain toward Bottom Town. He was lost in thought, but not so lost that he failed to notice the trap. On the ground sat a box, the same box as the first box Zach had used to trap him. Next to the box was a sign that read, "Look What's Inside."

"I'm not going to look in the box, Zach," said Geo loudly.

Zach came out from behind a tree and smiled at Geo. "Why not?" he asked.

Geo landed his bat, hopped off, and stood there staring at Zach. "Because," he said, "I don't feel like being trapped again."

"I promise there's something inside it this time," said Zach.

"No," said Geo firmly, "I won't look. Besides, why do you want to trap me again? I still don't have any shinies."

Zach walked over to Geo and sat down. "That's okay," he said. "I don't need them anymore."

"What? Why?" asked Geo. "Did you get picked?"

"I did," said Zach.

"Wow," said Geo. "How'd you get more stuff?"

"I didn't," said Zach. "After you left, I couldn't stop thinking about what you had done for me. I felt horrible. I couldn't believe what I'd done, or what I was willing to do, just to get picked. Then I began to wonder why I needed a pile of stuff to get picked in the first place. It seemed silly. A girl shouldn't want me for my stuff; she should want me for me. So, I decided to stand in line without any stuff."

"And you got picked?" asked Geo.

"Well," said Zach, "I didn't think I would at first. All the girls kept passing me by. I was about to leave when a girl walked up and asked me why I didn't have any stuff."

"What did you tell her?" asked Geo.

"I stared at her for a moment. Then I said, 'The reason I stand here, without any stuff, is that the girl who picks me ought to think I'm enough. Love's unconditioned; it comes with no fee. And, if I get picked, she should love me for me. My heart and my soul can't be piled up like gold, but they're what I'd give you as we both grow old. I'm honest, supportive, and trustworthy too. I'd build you up and support what you do. I'm kind in my actions and with what I say. The trust that you give me, I'll never betray. I'll be your equal, your partner, and friend—and I'll hold your hand as we walk toward the end. But, if you need stuff or to sit on a throne, then pick someone else. I'll be fine on my own. I promise to be the best man I can be, and that's what you'd get if you choose to pick me."

"Then what happened?" asked Geo.

"Well," said Zach, "she looked at me and smiled. Then she said, 'I've come here each season, and strangely enough, I've never seen someone without any stuff. Every boy brings it, some piled to the sky, but here is a secret between you and I. Stuff's like a fishing lure thrown in a creek, attracting the fish who are naive and weak... or like a trap in a giant bouquet, a cage with a lock so you can't fly away. I'm not much for status or bright, shiny things. I want a connection without any strings. You'd love me for me, as I would for you, supporting each other in all that we do. We'd grow together with each passing day, respecting the dreams we both bring on the way. I think that you're special, and different too, but you should pick me just as I should pick you.'"

"And that's when she picked you?" asked Geo.

"No," said Zach. "First we talked—we talked for hours—and by the end of the day we decided to pick each other."

"That's wonderful," said Geo. "But, why did you want to trap me again if you didn't need my shinies?"

Zach grinned, and then he reached into the box and pulled out a large bag that was hidden inside it. "I wanted to give you this," he said. "Before I went to the Picking Line, I returned all the stuff I had bought. I realized how important these were to you, and I wanted to give them back." Then he handed the bag to Geo. "Now maybe you can be happy again."

Geo opened the bag and saw that it was full of shinies. "My shinies!" he screamed, and then he began jumping up and down with excitement. "Thank you, Zach! Oh, thank you! Thank you! If I go back with these, then everyone will *have* to accept me again." Geo put the bag down and gave Zach a hug. Then, with his tail raised high, he slung the bag over his shoulder, climbed onto his bat, and flew back up the side of Mount Kerpuffin.

Back at the village under the rainbow, Geo opened his bag of shinies in front of Old Jasper and the rest of the Kerpuffins.

"Well done," said Old Jasper proudly. "You obviously learned your lesson."

The other Kerpuffins nodded in agreement.

"From this day on, Geo is no longer a Gunny," announced Old Jasper. "He truly understands that Kerpuffins are *nothing* without their shinies."

As the crowd of Kerpuffins clapped their hands together, Geo thought about Zach and the Picking Line. Then he asked himself, "*Why do I think I'm 'nothing' without shinies?*" It seemed silly to him. Then, the more he thought about it, the more he realized that Kerpuffins acted as silly as humans—if not sillier. "Wait," he said to them all. "I've changed my mind. I don't want any shinies."

The entire village of Kerpuffins went silent.

"What?" asked Old Jasper, uncertain of what he'd just heard.

"I said," said Geo, "'I don't want any shinies.'"

"Don't be silly," said Old Jasper. "Kerpuffins are *nothing* without their shinies. Without them you'll be a Gunny."

"No," said Geo. "Without them I'll be 'Geo.' Shinies don't change who I am, not deep down. I think I'd rather live on the other side of the mountain than live where I'm thought to be *nothing* without shinies." With that, he gave his bag of shinies to Old Jasper.

Then he climbed onto his bat, and they flew through the gem trees toward the other side of the mountain. As they did, Geo could hear the other Kerpuffins begin to argue with each other.

"Why would someone choose to live without shinies?" one of them asked.

"He said we don't need them," one of them answered.

"But we're *nothing* without shinies, right?" another one asked.

"I thought so," another one answered.

"Me too," said another.

"Are we?"

The last question caused several more arguments that were soon lost in the wind as Geo and his bat flew further away from the village. Soon the sun began to set below them, and above them the rainbow sparkled brightly against the darkening sky. As they made their way around the mountain, Geo began scratching at his chest. He looked down and realized that he was still wearing his gunnysack. He took it off, threw it into a cloud, and smiled.

"*Silly*," he thought.

Shortly before dawn, Geo found a Kerpuffin-sized footpath leading down the other side of the mountain. He and his bat followed it and came upon a forest of trees that grew leaves instead of jewels. It wasn't long before they saw something moving beneath the trees, several *somethings* in fact. They landed a short distance away and found that the *somethings* were Kerpuffins, just like Geo. And, just like Geo, none of them were wearing shinies, but none of them were wearing gunnysacks either. The Kerpuffins saw Geo and waved. As Geo waved back, a sense of peace filled his heart. For he knew he had found a place where he would be accepted for being himself—a Kerpuffin named Geo, who would never feel like *nothing* again.

That tale was a sweet one. The next one might be scary. It has a giant creature that's frightening and hairy. It sits outside a tree and waits there day and night. Let's read on and see why it's causing such a fright.

THE BUNDLETOOTH

———————

INSIDE A TREE LIVED THE TREEBRIGHTS. Although the Treebrights lived inside a tree, they were unaware that they lived inside it. "How could something not know it lived inside a tree?" you may ask. Well, imagine if your great, great, great ancestors built a village inside the trunk of a tree, and never left. Then imagine that their children never left... or their children... or their children, until everyone who lived inside the tree had forgotten they lived inside it.

"Why," you may ask, "did the Treebrights never leave the inside of that tree?" Well, you might think it was because the inside of that tree was quite a roomy place to be, considering the Treebrights grew to only inches of three. They resembled you or me, except for their big eyes, pointy ears, and snow-colored skin. They also had two tiny antennae that stuck out from the top of their head. They were so small that the tree in which they lived was large enough for a village where each of the Treebrights had a hut of their own. They ate bugs, which the tree provided more than enough of, and they drank water that dripped through the mud and bark. It was a perfect place for a Treebright to live, at least the Treebrights thought so, but that was not the reason why they never left. The reason they never left was because they were trapped.

What had trapped them in their tree? It was a thing so horrible, so terrible, and so terrifying that the Treebrights were afraid to leave the tree, until they'd forgotten the tree was something they could leave. The thing was ferocious. The thing was cunning. The thing was the most frightening thing in the history of frightening things. They called it—the *Bundletooth*.

A description of the Bundletooth had been written down to remind each new generation of Treebrights why *it* should be feared more than anything else they should fear, and it went like this:

"Beware the fearsome Bundletooth,
For it deceives and bends the truth.
A hundred teeth fill up its jaws.
Its feet have deadly sharpened claws.
It stuns you with hypnotic eyes.
It likes to dress up in disguise.
Its tail is sharp and poisonous too,
So, if you're stung, your life is through.
Its breath smells like old, rotten food.
Its manners are extremely rude.
Its mouth spits acid like a spout.
Its nose snorts fire from each snout.
Its growl will fill you full of dread.
It never cleans or makes its bed.
It's filled with hate and full of wrath.
It eats all those who cross its path.
Of all the things it likes to eat,
A Treebright is its favorite treat.
So, be afraid and don't forget
The Bundletooth may get you yet."

The only way the Bundletooth could reach the Treebrights was through a door that sat at the edge of their village. It was a

strong, sturdy door, but the Treebrights feared the Bundletooth might burst through it just the same. So, the door was barred, and signs were posted around it that read things like, "Danger," "Stay Back," and "Keep Out." Above the door, and much larger than the smaller signs, was a sign so big that it could be read from every hut in the village. "Beware the Bundletooth," it read, and so they did.

Like all the Treebrights, Wee, a young Treebright, was taught to fear the Bundletooth. But, unlike the other Treebrights, she feared the Bundletooth most of all.

Not too long ago, Wee's older sister, Blee, and a few other Treebrights had been digging a tunnel and looking for bugs. As they dug, Blee came across a rock and figured there might be some tasty bugs on the other side of it. As she pulled the rock from its place, something happened, something horrible. The tunnel began to shake. Dirt fell all around them. Then a blinding light shown through where the rock had been. The Treebrights screamed and ran away as fast as they could, believing they had dug a tunnel into the lair of the Bundletooth. There was a horrible roar, and the Treebrights barely managed to reach the village before the tunnel collapsed behind them. As they stood there shaken and scared, they realized that Wee's sister, Blee, was not with them and believed that she had been taken by the Bundletooth.

No Treebright had ever been taken by the Bundletooth, and Wee's loss of her older sister was a loss that no Treebright had ever felt. As time went on, Wee tried to do the things she always did, collecting bugs, bucketing water, and playing with her friends, though she could never get rid of the terrible feeling lodged in the middle of her chest. It was a painful feeling that stung just beneath the necklace she wore, which Blee had given to her. It had a stone in the center of it that hung against her heart. Wee held the rock in her tiny hand every time she thought of her sister, while sadly knowing that she would never see her sister again.

Not long after she lost Blee to the Bundletooth, Wee was leaving her hut to gather some water. She was alone. It was not quite yet morning, and everyone else was still sleeping. Mornings were different for Treebrights, though it wasn't how they woke up, or what they did after, that was different. Instead, it was the way that morning came, for mornings always arrived with the family of glowworms that lived above the Treebrights' village. The Treebrights called them "glowworms" because they glowed. They came and went through a very small hole, though where they went, and from where they came, the Treebrights didn't know. But each time the glowworms left, the village became dark; and each time they returned, the village became bright. When they left, the Treebrights went to sleep. When they returned, the Treebrights woke up.

By the time the glowworms returned that morning, Wee had found some water dripping near the door to the Bundletooth. As she drank, she heard a noise. It was a noise she had never heard before. Not knowing what the noise was or where it came from, she stood very still, waiting to hear it again; but all she could hear was the *drip, drip, drip* made by the water as it fell. After a while, she decided it was nothing and continued filling her bucket. Just as her bucket was almost full, she heard the noise again. Her body froze. Her eyes widened. Her mouth dropped open in a silent scream as she realized that the noise was coming from the other side of the door to the Bundletooth.

Knock. Knock. Knock.

Something was knocking on the other side of the door. Wee tried to scream, but her voice was caught in her throat.

Knock. Knock. Knock.

"It's come to get me!" she thought. She was so frightened that

her antennae stiffened, and her stomach began tying itself into knots. Then, without warning, a scream escaped from her throat and echoed through the village. It wasn't long before every Treebright came running to see what had happened.

"What is it?" asked one of them.

"What's going on?" asked another.

Wee was too frightened to speak. She just stared at them all, as they stared at her, until the knocking started again.

Knock. Knock. Knock.

The Treebrights panicked. Some of them screamed, some of them fainted, and some of them ran away.

"What's going on here?" asked Elderbright Snee, as he pushed his way through the crowed. The "Elderbrights" were the leaders of their village. There were three of them, and Elderbright Snee was the oldest and wisest of them all.

"It's the Bundletooth!" screamed one of the Treebrights.

"It's come to get us!" yelled another.

The knocking came again, only louder this time.

Knock. Knock. Knock.

Elderbright Snee tripped backward, almost falling over in fear. "It can't be," he said. "This has never happened before."

"What's never happened before?" asked Elderbright Zee, as she stepped calmly over a few of the fainted Treebrights and made her way through the crowd.

"Happened before what?" asked Elderbright Tee, as he followed Elderbright Zee. He wasn't as old as Elderbrights Snee or Zee, and he wasn't as wise either.

Elderbright Snee pointed a shaking finger toward the door and said, "It's the Bundletooth! It's come for us!"

Knock. Knock. Knock.

The Treebrights all screamed again. Then they heard something. It wasn't the sound of the Bundletooth's claws scratching, or its teeth gnashing, or its tail thrashing. Instead, to their surprise, it sounded like the voice of a girl.

"I'm not the Bundletooth," said the voice. "I'm a Treebright." This was followed by more knocking, but less screaming.

Elderbright Zee stared at the door curiously. "It says it's a Treebright," she said.

Elderbright Tee frowned. "That's not very likely," he said. "Treebrights live on this side of the door."

"That's right," said Elderbright Snee. "It could have changed its voice. It could be trying to trick us so that we'll open the door."

Then the voice spoke again. "I got lost," it said. "I've been trying to find my way back."

Elderbright Tee looked confused. "Way back from where?" he asked.

"It's speaking nonsense," said Elderbright Snee.

"Wait," said Wee, who had managed to find her voice again. Then she motioned for the rest of the Treebrights to quiet down. *"Could it be?"* she thought. *"Could it be?"* As the other Treebrights watched, she gathered what courage she had, stepped closer toward the door, and said, "Blee?...Blee, is that you?"

"Yes," said the voice from the other side of the door. "Wee, is that you?"

"Blee!" Wee yelled, as she began trying to unbar the door.

Elderbright Snee ran up to Wee and pulled her away. "What are you doing?" he asked, horrified. "You can't open the door. What if it's the Bundletooth?"

Wee shook herself loose from his grip. "It's not the Bundletooth," she said. "It's my sister. We have to let her in."

Elderbright Snee threw himself between Wee and the door. "Wait!" he yelled. "What if it's a trick? What if it's just *saying* it's Blee?"

Wee tried to push Elderbright Snee out of the way. "But, what if it *is* her?" she demanded. "What if she got away from the Bundletooth? What if it's after her? What if she needs help?"

Elderbright Snee grabbed Wee's hand and pulled her away from the door. "We can't be sure. And, since we can't be sure, the door stays closed."

Wee thought about this for a moment. Then she touched her necklace. "Wait," she said. "What if we *could* be sure? What if I asked her a question only she would know?"

Elderbright Snee squinted his eyes at her. "Like what?" he asked.

"Like this," said Wee. She shook loose from Elderbright Snee's hand and turned toward the door to the Bundletooth. Then she took off her necklace, held it in front of her, and said, "Blee, if it *is* you, then tell me what I'm holding in my hand. You gave it to me just before the Bundletooth got you."

Every Treebright who had not fainted, or run away, listened closely for the answer. After a few moments of silence, the answer came.

"It's the necklace," said the voice. "The necklace with the stone I gave you."

Wee jumped with excitement. "See," she said to the Elderbrights. "It *is* her!"

The crowd of Treebrights began mumbling to each other. Then one of them said, "Let her back in!" This was followed by the voice of several others. "Let her back in! Let her back in!"

"Please," said Wee, "please open the door. She could be in trouble."

As the chanting grew louder, the Elderbrights huddled together and began whispering to each other. Then Elderbright Snee turned back toward the crowd and raised his hands to calm them down. "If we open the door," he said to them, "then we could be risking our lives. But, if we don't, then we could be leaving one of our own to be eaten by the Bundletooth, and we believe the memory of that would be worse than death." He furrowed his brow, shook his head, and said, "So, we've decided to open the door." With that, the Elderbrights began unbarring the door to the Bundletooth.

Wee waited anxiously. She knew it must be her sister; she just knew it. The rest of the Treebrights didn't seem so sure, and they began to back away from the door. As the last bar was removed, the Elderbrights stepped back when, for the first time since it was closed, the door to the Bundletooth began to open.

Every Treebright, including Wee, held their breath as something emerged from the other side of the door. It was small, like them, but it was so dark that it was difficult to be sure of what it was.

"Blee?" asked Wee, uncertainly. She thought it was her, but the shadows were making it difficult to see.

As the figure emerged from the darkness, the Treebrights gasped at what they saw. It *was* Blee, but her skin was glistening. Her hair had changed too; it was much lighter than before. But, what had changed the most were her eyes. They were sparkling.

Before Wee could ask what had happened, the Elderbrights quickly closed the door to the Bundletooth and began to bar it shut.

"Wait," said Blee to the Elderbrights. "You don't have to do that."

Elderbright Snee turned toward Blee as he pushed the last bar in place. "Of course, we do," he said. "The Bundletooth could get in."

Blee started to say something, but she was interrupted when Wee ran up and hugged her.

"You're alive," said Wee. "Where were you? What happened to your skin? Did the Bundletooth breathe on you?"

Before Blee could answer, a young Treebright stepped out from the crowd. "And what happened to your hair?" he asked. "Did the Bundletooth lick you with its acidic tongue?"

Then another Treebright stepped forward. "What happened to your eyes?" she asked. "Did you look into the Bundletooth's fearsome stare?"

"No," said Blee to them. "It was the light. The light did this to me."

"What light?" asked Wee.

Blee took her sister's hand in hers, and then she turned to face the crowd. "I saw a light that's brighter than the brightest light you've ever seen. That's why I tried to find my way back. I wanted to tell you what I saw. It was amazing, like nothing you've ever imagined." Then she turned and hugged Wee again. "I'm sorry that I've been gone so long. I couldn't find a way back in."

Wee drew back from her sister, confused. "What do you mean?" she asked. "'Back in' from where?"

Blee smiled at Wee and said, "When I was digging, the tunnel caved in, and I suddenly found myself somewhere we never knew was there. It's like nothing we've known. It's... 'Unknown.'"

Elderbright Snee huffed as he stepped in between Blee and the crowd. "And just where *is* this 'Unknown?'" he asked.

"Out there," said Blee. "It's what's outside this tree."

"What's a tree?" asked Elderbright Tee.

Blee pointed toward the walls around their village. "It's what we're living in," she said.

Elderbright Tee stared at her blankly. "I don't understand," he said, and neither did any of the other Treebrights.

"It's hard to describe," said Blee. "It's different. It's big. It's like nothing you've ever seen. We don't have the words to describe it. You'd have to see it for yourself."

"What?" asked Elderbright Snee. "You mean go through the door?"

"Yes," said Blee. "That's why I didn't want you to close it. I want you to see it. I want all of you to see it... it's amazing. It's..."

"Ridiculous," said Elderbright Snee. "We can't go through the door. The Bundletooth will get us."

"No," said Blee. "That's what I wanted to tell you." And what she told them next shocked the ears of every Treebright who heard it. She looked at them all. Then she took in a deep breath and said, "There is no Bundletooth."

The silence that followed was deafening, leaving only the sound of her words echoing off the walls. It was Elderbright Zee who finally broke the silence.

"My dear child," she said softly, "it's obvious you've been through something horrible. You just need some time to rest. Your sister can take you home. I'm sure you'll find yourself thinking more clearly tomorrow."

Elderbright Snee patted Blee on the shoulder as he turned toward the crowd. "That's right," he announced to them all. "She just needs some rest. She's been through a very upsetting ordeal."

Blee took a step away from him and shook her head. "But I haven't. It wasn't horrible or upsetting. At first it was confusing, but once I saw things more clearly, I couldn't believe what I saw. It wasn't the Bundletooth. It was beautiful."

Elderbright Snee shook his head furiously. "No," he said. "There *is* a Bundletooth, and it's on the other side of that door."

Elderbright Tee pointed toward the sign above the door. "The sign says so," he said, though he read it again to make sure.

"Then why didn't it eat me?" Blee asked them.

"Simple," said Elderbright Snee. "It could have been hiding somewhere, hoping you'd come back here and tell us that it doesn't exist. Then it would wait to eat us when we follow you back through the door."

"I promise you," said Blee. "There is no Bundletooth."

The crowd became uneasy again. Then someone said, "Perhaps it hypnotized you with its hypnotic eyes." Then someone else said, "Perhaps it was wearing a good disguise." Then someone else said, "It could have poisoned your mind with its poisonous tail."

Elderbright Snee nodded and said, "Which made you come back and tell us this tale."

"None of that's true," said Blee. "Nothing happened to me. There is no Bundletooth."

Elderbright Snee threw his hands in the air. "Madness!" he said to the crowd. "Her mind has gone mad!" Then he turned toward Blee. "What are you trying to do? Get us killed? The Bundletooth would like nothing more than for us to walk through that door. Then it would use its huge teeth to gnash us to bits or fry us alive with the acid it spits. It would crush us beneath its huge, heavy paws or scratch us to death with its sharp, jagged claws. It would tell us all lies in soft, soothing tones and then pick its teeth clean with what's left of our bones." Then he turned back to the crowd. "No!" he yelled. "The Bundletooth is real. Mark my words, any one of you who walks through that door is doomed!"

Blee looked down at Wee, who had let go of her hand. "You believe me? Don't you?"

Wee looked up at Blee, not knowing what to say. "*There has to be a Bundletooth*," she thought. "*Hasn't there?*"

Elderbright Snee clapped his hands together to get everyone's attention. "The Bundletooth *is* real, and it sent her back to confuse us with doubt. But, I tell you this, we will not be fooled by the Bundletooth." Then his eyes widened, as if frightened by a thought. He took a few steps away from Blee and pointed his finger at her. "Or," he said fearfully, "is it possible we've

already been fooled? Look at her skin. Look at her hair. Look at her eyes. She could be the Bundletooth wearing a disguise!"

The Treebrights began screaming again, realizing the thing they feared most could be standing right in front of them.

"No!" said Wee. "It's Blee! I know it is," at least she thought she did. She didn't know what to think anymore, and neither did the rest of the Treebrights. They all started backing away from Blee, as if she might sprout sharp, jagged claws, poisonous teeth, or bone-crushing paws. Some kept screaming and some ran away, afraid she'd snort fire or had acid to spray.

Elderbright Snee raised his hands in an effort to calm them down. "Go back to your huts!" he yelled. "Your Elderbrights will take care of this."

"How?" asked Elderbright Tee, as the rest of the Treebrights ran screaming toward their huts. "She could kill us all right now."

"I'm *not* the Bundletooth," insisted Blee, though her voice was drowned out by everyone's screams.

Elderbright Zee didn't seem as afraid as the others. Instead of screaming, she patted Blee on the shoulder and said calmly, "It's okay dear. We believe you."

"What?" asked Elderbright Snee.

"We do?" asked Elderbright Tee.

Elderbright Zee grabbed Elderbright Snee. Then she pulled him close, so no one could hear them, and said, "Look, if she is the Bundletooth, then perhaps we should go along with it. Otherwise, she'll eat us right now."

"So," said Elderbright Snee, "you're saying it would be better if she ate us later?"

Elderbright Tee nodded his head as he joined them. "I think so," he said.

"Fine," said Elderbright Snee. "Then what should we do?"

The Elderbrights huddled together, whispered to each other, and then nodded their heads. After a few more whispers, Elderbright Snee turned around to face Blee. "We've decided that we need to hear more about this 'Unknown.'"

Blee looked relieved. "So, you believe me?"

Elderbright Zee smiled a friendly smile and said, "Of course we do dear. Now, why don't you follow us and tell us more about where you've been."

Wee, who was still standing beside her sister, asked if she could come too.

Elderbright Zee looked down at Wee and said, "Not now... This is Elder talk, but we won't be long."

With that, Wee watched as the Elderbrights led Blee toward the other side of the village. When they were gone from sight, Wee just stood there, not knowing what else to do. Finally, the Elderbrights returned, but without Blee.

Wee tried to stop them as they passed her. "Where is she? Where'd she go?"

Elderbright Zee stopped as the others kept walking. "Don't worry about it. You're safe now. We put it in a cage."

"What?" asked Wee, horrified. "You put her in a cage?"

"Yes," said Elderbright Zee, "to protect us... to protect you." Then, seeing that Wee was upset, she bent down to give her a hug. After a moment, she drew back, looked into Wee's eyes, and said, "You need to go to your hut now. Your Elderbrights need time to talk this over." Then she stood up, patted Wee on the head, and rushed off to catch up with the other Elderbrights.

As the Elderbrights walked out of sight, Wee decided not to go back to her hut. Instead, she followed them, making sure she stayed far enough behind so as not to be seen. She wasn't worried about losing them. She figured they were heading to the "Knowledge Hut." It was where the Elderbrights always discussed important things. A few moments later, she saw them go into the Knowledge Hut and then close the door behind them.

Wee waited until she was sure they had time to settle in. Then she crept up to the Knowledge Hut and peeked in through a crack between the door and the frame. The inside of the hut was lined with shelves. Every important event that happened to the Treebrights was carved into wood and stored on those shelves. The Elderbrights were sitting at a table in the center of the room. Elderbright Zee was busy carving that day's events onto a new piece of wood while

Elderbright's Snee and Tee argued with each other about what to do next.

"For the last time," said Elderbright Snee, "we're not going to set her on fire."

"Why?" asked Elderbright Tee. "The Bundletooth can't be burned. So, if we set her on fire, then we'll know if she's the Bundletooth."

Elderbright Snee sighed a deep sigh and said, "If she isn't the Bundletooth, then she'll be burned."

"But," said Elderbright Tee, "what if she *is* the Bundletooth?"

Elderbright Zee looked up from her carving, rolled her eyes, and said, "Then you'll probably have just made it very angry."

Elderbright Snee agreed with her. "We'll have to think of something else," he said.

Elderbright Tee thought for a moment. "How about water?" he asked. "The Bundletooth can breathe under water. If we throw her into a pool and hold her under…"

"No," said Elderbright Snee. "We're not going to drown her either."

"But," said Elderbright Tee, "it won't drown if it's the Bundletooth."

"And again," said Elderbright Zee, "you'll have just made it very angry."

Elderbright Snee rubbed his face with his hands. "There has to be something we can do. There has to be some kind of test that won't kill her or make it angry."

Elderbright Zee looked up from her woodcarving. "If it really is the Bundletooth, then I don't understand why it doesn't just eat us now and get it over with."

"Because," said Elderbright Snee, "it could be toying with us. You know, playing with its food."

"You really think so?" asked Elderbright Zee. "It *is* still possible that it's Blee, and not the Bundletooth. That would make more sense."

Elderbright Snee nodded his head. "It would," he said, "but if that's the case, then the Bundletooth must obviously be controlling her. Why else would she say it doesn't exist?"

There was silence for a moment. Then Elderbright Zee said, "What if it doesn't exist? What if she's right?"

Elderbright Tee gasped. "It has to exist," he said. "I'd hate to think I've been afraid all these years for no reason."

Elderbright Snee stood up and pounded his fist on the table.

"This is exactly what it wants us to do," he said. "It's filling our heads full of questions, and questions bring nothing but trouble. One question just leads to another. It never ends. That's why we have answers. Answers are better. They put a nice cap on the whole thing. Questions are more like a leaky roof—drip, drip, drip, one after another. They keep you up at night, and eventually you'll go mad, wishing you could stop the noise."

He stopped for a moment and then leaned forward toward the other two. "Blee is like a leaky roof. She needs to be stopped. Once you start questioning the answers, the whole thing falls apart. That's what the Bundletooth wants. It wants us to question its existence. The second we stop believing it exists, we'll get shredded by its claws, or chewed in its jaws, or…"

"So, what do we do?" asked Elderbright Zee, impatiently.

"Well," said Elderbright Snee, "how do you fix a leaky roof?"

Elderbright Tee thought for a moment. "Put mud on it?"

"I don't see how that would help," said Elderbright Zee.

"We're not putting mud on her," said Elderbright Snee. "We just need to find a way to 'un-hypnotize' her so that she doesn't keep trying to fill our minds with questions.

Elderbright Zee looked up from her carving. "So, how should we move forward?"

Elderbright Snee grunted and sat back down. "That's the problem. It probably wants us to move forward. It wants us to do something we've never done. That's how it starts. We've always been safe going around in a circle. A circle is comfortable. We know where we've been, and we know where we're going. Each generation keeps the circle going for the next generation. It keeps us safe, it gives us focus, and it protects us from the Bundletooth."

"So, again," said Elderbright Zee, "what do we do? It sounds like anything we try could just make it worse."

"We could try doing nothing," said Elderbright Tee.

"No," said Elderbright Snee, "we have to do something. It would want us to do nothing."

Elderbright Tee looked confused. "I thought you said it wanted us to move forward."

Elderbright Snee began pulling on his antenna, a sure sign that he was frustrated. "We should have never opened that door," he said bitterly. There was silence again. Then, all at once, Elderbright Snee stood up and clapped his hands together so loudly that it startled the other two. "That's it," he said. "I've got it. What if we don't open the door?"

Elderbright Tee looked confused again. "But we already opened it," he said.

Elderbright Zee nodded her head and held up her woodcarving. "I even carved it down," she said.

Elderbright Snee smiled and sat down again. "Everyone only *thinks* we opened the door. What if everyone thought we *didn't* open it?"

Elderbright Zee stared at him. "Why would they think that?" she asked.

"Because," he said, "we'll tell them that it was never opened."

Elderbright Zee shook her head. "But they were there. They saw it open."

"No," said Elderbright Snee, "they only *thought* they saw it open."

Elderbright Tee's expression went from confused to baffled and then finally settled on perplexed. "I thought I saw it open too," he said.

"Exactly," said Elderbright Snee, "but thoughts are just thoughts. What if we told everyone the whole thing was just a dream, some kind of mass hypnosis created by the Bundletooth to make us question its existence?"

Elderbright Zee gave him a long, steady look. "Would they believe us?"

"Of course, they would," said Elderbright Snee. "Why wouldn't they?"

Elderbright Zee frowned and began fiddling with her woodcarving. "But then we would be... We'd be lying."

"True," said Elderbright Snee, "but only to protect them, which makes it okay."

"I guess so," said Elderbright Zee. "But what would we do with Blee?"

Elderbright Snee thought for a moment. Then he said, "She should stay in her cage. We'll put the cage in here until we figure out what to do with her. That way everyone will think that she never came back. They'll have no reason not to believe us."

"In here?" asked Elderbright Tee. "But what if she *is* the Bundletooth?"

Elderbright Zee grinned a little and said, "Well, if she is the Bundletooth, then we'll probably be dead by morning and none of this will matter."

Elderbright Tee sank in his chair. "Well, that's not very reassuring."

Elderbrights Snee and Zee agreed, but it seemed they had no other choice.

"Then it's settled," said Elderbright Snee. "We'll retrieve Blee, along with her cage, and put both of them in here. Then, unless we're all dead by morning, we'll announce to everyone that it was just a dream created by the Bundletooth. This should settle everyone down while we figure out what to do next."

Elderbright Zee looked down at her woodcarving. "What do I do with this?" she asked.

Elderbright Snee stared at it. "Destroy it," he said. "This never happened."

With that, Wee watched as the three of them stood up from the table and walked toward the door. She quickly ducked around the side of the hut before the Elderbrights opened the door and stepped outside. They muttered something to each other before walking off and disappearing around the corner. Wee thought about following them but decided to wait.

As the glowworms began to leave and the light began to fade, she watched as the Elderbrights returned, carrying Blee in a cage. Wee ducked behind the Knowledge Hut, as they opened the door and put Blee inside. She could hear her sister protesting as they walked back out of the hut, closing the door behind them. The Elderbrights stood there for a moment while looking out over the village. Then Elderbright Snee took in a deep breath and spoke so loudly that every Treebright in every hut could hear him. He told the Treebrights that they should spend the rest of the night in their huts and that their Elderbrights would have more answers for them in the morning. When he finished, the Elderbrights walked back to their own huts to wait for the glowworms' return.

The village became dark, and the only noise that could be heard was the *drip, drip, drip* of water falling in puddles on the ground. Wee could also hear the sound of sobs coming from inside the Knowledge Hut. As her eyes adjusted to the dark, Wee peeked through the door and found her sister sitting in the cage. At least it

looked like her sister, but after everything the Elderbrights had said, Wee was afraid that what looked like her sister could, in fact, be the Bundletooth. *"But, why would the Bundletooth be crying?"* she asked herself. She knew she couldn't just stand there doing nothing, so she decided to whisper her sister's name through the door.

"Blee?"

The sobbing stopped. "Wee? Is that you?" The voice sounded anxious. "Can you get me out of here? They've gone mad. They think I'm the Bundletooth."

"I know," said Wee, but then she thought, *"Maybe I've gone mad. I could be talking to the Bundletooth—or is it my sister?"* She didn't know. All she knew was that she felt frightened and unsure of what to do next.

Then, whatever was in the cage started crying again and said, "I thought everyone would be happy. I thought, if I came back and explained what I saw, they would want to see it for themselves."

"What did you see?" asked Wee, who had opened the door a little bit more, so she could see the cage more clearly.

"I can't really describe it. We have no words for it, but when I saw what I saw, I realized I knew nothing. Suddenly, everything I believed in wasn't true. At first I went mad. I didn't know what was real and what wasn't. Everywhere I looked was something new, a new way to see, a new way to think, a new way to be... It was amazing, and confusing, and it took me awhile to take it all in. When my mind finally began to settle down, I wanted to come back here and tell everyone—tell you—about the Unknown. But, everyone believes in the Bundletooth, and I didn't consider how I was asking everyone to stop believing in everything they believe. I wasn't thinking. Of course they're afraid of me. I would be too. And now they think I'm the Bundletooth."

Wee could hear more crying coming from inside the hut, and she knew, with all of her heart, that this was not the Bundletooth. Before another second passed, Wee threw open the door and ran to her sister. Then she opened the cage, reached inside, and hugged her.

Her sister, who was not the Bundletooth, hugged her back.

"You believe me," said Blee, still crying.

"I do," said Wee, who had started crying herself.

They both held each other and cried until they had no tears left. Then Blee pulled back and looked down at Wee. "What's going to happen now?"

"I'm not sure," said Wee. "I heard them talking," and she told Blee what the Elderbrights were planning to do.

"I didn't mean to upset everyone," said Blee. "But, the Elderbrights are right. One question *does* lead to another. My mind is full of them. Now I almost wish I hadn't seen the Unknown."

Wee sat back and shook her head. "No," she said, "if you're right, and there really isn't a Bundletooth, then I've spent my whole life being afraid of something that doesn't exist. If that's true, then I would rather have a head full of questions than live my life afraid of the Bundletooth." She paused for a moment and then asked, "Will you take me to the Unknown?"

"Are you sure?" asked Blee. "If you see it, then everything you believe will disappear."

Wee thought about it. She could stay in their village, she could try to forget, but the question would always be there: *"Is there a Bundletooth?"* She knew then that the answer to that question would be worth all of the questions that followed it. "Yes," she said finally, "I'm sure."

"Okay then," said Blee, "I'll take you."

As they left the Knowledge Hut, the rest of the village seemed sound asleep. Blee and Wee stepped quietly and carefully, so as not to wake anyone. While they made their way toward the door to the Bundletooth, Wee couldn't help but feel frightened as the words from the poem began drifting through her thoughts.

A hundred teeth fill up its jaws…

Soon they reached the door with all of its warning signs begging them to stop what they were about to do.

Its feet have deadly sharpened claws…

Slowly, and with all of their strength, they managed to unbar the door.

Its tail is sharp and poisonous too…

Then Blee grabbed the door handle and pulled with all of her might.

So, if you're stung, your life is through…

The door began to open.

So, be afraid and don't forget…

Wee stepped back.

The Bundletooth may get you yet.

…but nothing was there.

Instead of the Bundletooth, Wee saw a tunnel trailing off into the dark.

"Last chance," said Blee, as she turned and looked at Wee. "Are you sure you want to come?"

Wee wasn't sure of anything at the moment. Elderbright Snee had been right; moving forward was more frightening than going around in a circle. She stood there, facing her deepest fear, and finally gathered up enough courage to step forward. "Yes," she said to Blee, "I'm sure." Then she stepped forward again.

Blee took Wee's hand in hers and led her into the tunnel. It was so dark that Wee was unable to see much of anything except for the faint glow of her sister's skin. She could feel the muddy ground beneath her feet and Blee's hand holding onto hers. Then she felt something else, like something was breathing on her.

Its breath smells like old, rotten food...

Wee almost screamed, but she realized it didn't smell like rotten food at all. Instead, it smelled almost pleasant and sweet. The smell got stronger as they continued moving forward. Then, all at once, Wee saw a tiny light glowing ahead of them. She stopped and froze where she stood.

Its nose snorts fire from each snout...

"It's okay," said Blee. "It's the 'Light.' It's nothing to be afraid of."

Wee felt Blee grip her hand reassuringly.

"We can go back if you want," said Blee.

Wee knew there was no going back, so she took in a deep breath and took another step forward. Then she took another. Slowly, one step after the other, Wee followed Blee toward the light, which got brighter with each step they took. The tunnel got warmer too, and Wee could hear noises coming from the light—sounds she had never heard before. As they began climbing upward, Wee saw that the light was coming through a hole that was not much wider than they were.

"That's it," said Blee. "That's the Unknown."

Wee could feel warmth coming from the other side of the hole. It felt amazing, like nothing she had ever felt before.

"I'll go first," said Blee. Then she stepped through the hole and into the light.

Wee watched as the light reflected off her sister. It made her skin glow brighter and her eyes sparkle. Blee smiled and reached down for Wee's hand. Wee took her sister's hand, took in a deep

breath, and began pulling herself up and out of the hole. The light grew brighter. The smells grew stronger. The sounds grew louder. Then, with one more step, she climbed out of the hole and into the light.

Her eyes widened.

Her mouth dropped open.

Her mind became an explosion of questions.

She started giggling at the sight of it all. Then she felt like crying, and tears began to fall from her eyes. She fell to her knees as the light, brighter than the brightest light she had ever imagined, enveloped her with warmth. Everything she saw, everything she felt, and everything she heard had no words to describe it. Wee held onto her sister's hand tightly as everything she believed, and everything she feared, vanished in the light of the Unknown.

That morning, as the glowworms returned, the Treebrights found that the door to the Bundletooth was open. The Elderbrights came and closed the door as quickly as they could. Then they barred it shut and even covered it with a wall of rocks. But, no matter what the Elderbrights did, no matter what the Elderbrights said, every Treebright in that tree couldn't help but question to some degree:

"Is there a Bundletooth?"

That was kind of scary. The next one's much less frightful. There's a castle made of candy, and it's said to taste delightful. Its maker is beguiling. He never works for free. How much would his castle cost? Let's read on and see.

THE CANDY CASTLE MAKER

THE WINTER COLD WAS COMING; all the signs were there. Leaves were brown and falling down through the chilly air. The foxes made their burrows; the rabbits dug their holes, as did all the groundhogs, badgers, skunks, and moles. The birds flew south. The bears made beds. Beavers built their dams. The humans cut up firewood and set up jellied jams. Soon creeks would freeze, as would the breeze, when temperatures dropped low, and the town of Hidden Hollow would soon be filled with snow. Those who lived there never knew how long the cold would last, so they stored up what they could to wait until it passed. They traded with each other for the things that they might need, with no sign of selfishness, thievery, or greed. Because of this, the townsfolk always made it to the spring, until one fall the balance broke and threw off everything.

"Do I have to?" asked Weebundle, as an itchy woolen sweater was pulled over his head.

"Yes," said Granny Mum, "it's good for you."

Weebundle, though he was only five years old, often disagreed with what Granny Mum considered "good for him." While she thought the itchy woolen sweater was good for him, he

thought it itched worse than a bad case of poison ivy.

"The chill is getting stronger," said Granny Mum. "I don't want you catching a cold on your way to town."

"I know," said Weebundle, "but it itches." Then he scratched at his neck to make his point more clear.

"Blame the sheep, not me," said Granny Mum. She pulled his left hand through the sleeve as he continued scratching at his neck with his other hand. "When you stop growing so fast, I'll trade for some proper clothes. Until then, this will have to do." Then she chuckled as she watched him scratch at the sweater. She always chuckled at him; she chuckled at everything. She was a plump, roundish woman, older than she could remember, who believed chuckling was a pleasant way to spend the day. When she wasn't chuckling, she was smiling to herself as she worked around their farm. They called it a "farm," but it was really nothing more than an old cottage with a small barn off to the side. There were a few shearing sheep, some laying hens, and a milking goat. In the spring, the farm looked like a flowering paradise, and Granny Mum would spend most of her free time stooped over her flower gardens. She gave each flower all the love and care that she gave to everything, except for Weebundle, who she loved and cared for the most.

Weebundle loved Granny Mum as much as she loved him, and he hardly complained about anything, except for her sweaters. He often helped her around the farm and made trips to the town of Hidden Hollow, where he traded for things they needed. Granny Mum used to make the trips with him, but the path through the woods had become difficult for her. So, Weebundle began making the trips alone. He was happy to do it. She had been kind enough to raise him, and he would do more for her if he could. But being only five years old, he was limited in the things he could do.

At least he *thought* he was five years old. It had been five years since Granny Mum found him on her doorstep. She told him that he had been bundled up in a wee basket, and so she nicknamed him "Weebundle." When he was old enough to ask Granny Mum what his real name was, she had forgotten it, and so "Weebundle" became his name.

That morning, after Granny Mum finished with his sweater, she helped load a stack of hand-sewn quilts and woolly sweaters onto Weebundle's pull wagon.

"Now you be careful on your way to town," she said with warning. "Remember, the woods are full of tricky things this time of year."

"I'll be careful," said Weebundle.

Granny Mum kissed him on the cheek, gave him some bread to eat on the way, and said, "Be back before dark."

"I will," he said, grabbing the wagon's handle. Then he headed down the path that led through the woods and toward the town of Hidden Hollow.

The trees along the path were almost bare. The woods were quiet, except for an occasional rustling in the fallen leaves. Weebundle was not afraid of the forest, no matter what Granny Mum said was in it. In fact, when she was napping, he often went to a secret place just off the path about halfway to town. It was in a small meadow, hidden by a clump of trees. In the center of the meadow, was a giant rock that Weebundle could lie on and watch the clouds go by. In the spring and summer, the meadow was full of wild flowers.

That morning, as Weebundle stopped there to take off his woolen sweater, he found the meadow covered in a blanket of red and orange leaves. The leaves looked fun to jump through, but he

had no time to play that day. Instead, he just removed the sweater and threw it in his wagon. After scratching his neck a few times, he left his secret meadow and continued on his way to town.

As Weebundle and his wagon came to the top of a hill, he could see the town of Hidden Hollow nestled in the trees below. It wasn't a very big town. Only one road ran through it, along which sat a few shops, a café, and an inn. Most of the farmers in the area came there to trade, and autumn was the busiest trading time of the year. The street was full of people, and Weebundle found it difficult to make his way through the crowd. Granny Mum had given him a list of three shops to visit. The first was Miss Wick's candle shop, followed by Mr. Chop's wood shop, and finally Miss Prune's preserves shop. He traded Miss Wick a quilt for some candles. He traded Mr. Chop some sweaters for a delivery of firewood. Then he traded what he had left for some jars of Miss Prune's preserves. After that, he headed back home.

Along the way, Weebundle stopped at his secret meadow to put on his woolly sweater, which seemed to itch more than before. Just as he pulled his arms through the sleeves, he heard a cough. Startled, he looked up to find someone lying on the rock that sat in the center of the meadow. It looked more like a some-*thing* rather than a some-*one*, like a short, thin man, but not a man at all. He had a pointed chin. His hair was grey and thin. A long, gigantic nose sat above a pompous grin. His ears looked like a donkey's. His eyebrows were too thick, which he groomed with lots of wax to make them both look slick. His eyes were too wide, and fingers too long. His tiny, black suit seemed to fit him all wrong. His feet were bound tight in some black, buckled shoes, and the whole of him looked like a bunch of bad news.

He was truly an odd-looking creature, and he seemed like something Granny Mum would warn about. She had spent many nights filling Weebundle's imagination with creatures that roamed the forest, creatures full of trickery that wanted nothing more than to wreak havoc on humans. She had said that if he saw one, he should just keep on walking, and so he did.

"Wait a moment," said the creature. "Aren't you going to introduce yourself?"

"No," said Weebundle, "Granny Mum says I'm not supposed to talk to creatures like you."

The creature laughed. "Then your Granny Mum is a very smart woman," he said. His voice had smoothness to it, as if it had been polished to the point of shining. "The forest is full of rascals, and swindlers, and charmers of all kinds, but I am not one of them. I assure you."

"Why should I believe you?" asked Weebundle.

The creature laughed again. "Because," he said dramatically, "unlike them, I have a profession. And it happens to be the most amazing profession a profession can be."

Weebundle stopped walking. He knew Granny Mum would want him to keep going, but he found himself curious, so he turned back around. "What profession?" he asked.

The creature clapped his hands together and stood up on the rock. "Now that is a good question," he said, "a good question indeed. The answer to which is most incredible, so incredible, in fact, that I can only whisper it, for fear of causing a stampede of people wanting to buy the wonderful things that I make." The creature thought for a moment. Then he snapped his fingers and said, "I tell you what, if you come closer, then I will whisper to you what it is that I do."

Weebundle scratched at his woolen sweater, decided to ignore Granny Mum, and began pulling his wagon toward the rock.

"That's better," said the creature happily. "But, before I tell you what I do, first I will tell you who I am, because who I am is someone you will want to know." The creature took in a deep breath, raised his hand into the air, and said boastfully, "I am known as… and my name is… Mr. Inveiglebluff."

"Mr. what?" asked Weebundle, not sure he'd heard it correctly.

"Mr. In-veigle-bluff," said Mr. Inveiglebluff, "but if you give me one of those peaches in one of those jars, I will tell you my nickname as well."

"I can't," said Weebundle. "Granny Mum said we need these to get through the winter."

"Of course, you do," said Mr. Inveiglebluff, "but I doubt if the loss of one peach will cause you to starve. Besides, a nickname is worth far more than one peach. A nickname establishes friendship, a rapport—trust. Certainly all of that is worth one single peach."

Weebundle thought it over and decided one peach wouldn't hurt. So, he opened a jar of Miss Prune's preserves and handed Mr. Inveiglebluff a single peach. "They don't taste very good," said Weebundle, "but Granny Mum says they can last till the end of winter, which is why she always hopes the winter won't last very long."

Mr. Inveiglebluff held the peach between his long, pointy fingers and then dropped it into his mouth. After swallowing it, he grimaced and said, "I should have charged you two peaches considering the taste of the one." Then he sat back down on the rock and cleared his throat. "My nickname," he said, "is known only to my friends. After you know it, you must promise to keep it a secret—whatever you do. Is that understood?"

Weebundle nodded.

"Good," said Mr. Inveiglebluff. "Now that we're in agreement, I can tell you that my nickname is…" He paused, tilted his head toward the sky dramatically, and said, "Veigle." He grinned and looked back down at Weebundle. "Now that you know it, you may also call me by it." Veigle made his last statement sound like such an honor that Weebundle thanked him. "You're welcome," said Veigle.

There was silence for a moment until Weebundle finally said, "Well?"

"Well what?" asked Veigle, still licking the peach juice from his fingertips.

"Aren't you going to tell me what you do?"

"I will," said Veigle, "but that will cost you another peach."

"What?" asked Weebundle. "I just gave you one."

"True," said Veigle. "But a reveal of this magnitude is certainly worth another peach. Actually, it's worth two peaches, but I'm willing to reveal it today, this very moment, for one single peach. I'd say that's quite a deal, wouldn't you?"

"I guess so," said Weebundle. Then he opened the jar and gave Veigle another peach.

Veigle sucked the peach down as quickly as the last. Then he smacked his lips together and reached into a large, brown satchel sitting beside him. He dug through it until he pulled out a glass object, as round as a ball and the size of an apple. Then he held the object in front of Weebundle. "My boy," he said, as he pointed toward the object with his long, pointy finger, "I am proud to say, with absolutely no modesty or humility, that I, Veigle, am a builder of these."

"You make glass balls?" asked Weebundle. "I don't see what's so special about that."

"No," said Veigle. "I make what's inside the ball." Then he held it closer to Weebundle and tapped it with his finger. "Just look inside and you will see the most amazing thing a thing could be."

Weebundle looked into the glass ball, and his eyes widened at what he saw. Inside the ball was a castle, though it was unlike any castle he had ever seen because, unlike other castles, this castle was made out of candy.

"Amazing, isn't it." said Veigle.

Weebundle nodded his head. It was amazing, so amazing that he would have stared at it all day if Veigle hadn't placed it back in his satchel.

After Veigle put the satchel down, he grinned and said, "And, my boy, it tastes like everything you've wished you could taste."

"How do you taste it through the glass?" asked Weebundle.

Veigle laughed. "That was only a model. The castles I build are as tall as these trees and as wide as this meadow. I could tell you more, but not for free. Another peach, or perhaps even two, and I'll explain how I make them to you. Actually, it's so incredible I should be asking for three, but for you, I'll ask for just two."

Even more curious than before, Weebundle opened the jar, took out two more peaches, and handed them to Veigle who sucked them down with a lip-smacking *slurp*.

"A candied castle is really quite a treat," he began, as he licked the juice off his fingertips. "Its craftsmanship and quality simply can't be beat. It's astounding and confounding, a marvel through and through. Listen up, and I'll explain just how they're made to you." Then Veigle cleared his throat, stood up proudly, and gestured toward the sky. "I use a little magic and just a pinch of flair, a spoonful of compassion, some tenderness, and care. A cup of golden sunshine and some dewdrops do the trick, plus pounds and pounds of sugar... enough to make you sick. Then I put them in a pot, heat it till it's hot, and stir until it's all dissolved, with all the strength I've got. Then it's stretched and shaped, with flavor in the mix, for raspberry-flavored columns and lemon-flavored bricks. There's strawberry-flavored windows and root beer-flavored doors, a flavor for each step you take across its candied floors. The barrels made of butterscotch are a true delight, and the coffee-flavored fixtures often keep you up at night. The sugar on its rooftop always sparkles in the sun. Each vase is filled with lollypops, each different, every one. Its candied spears, curls, and sticks are marvels you must see. It's really quite amazing, and nothing's sugar free.

"But, the best part of it all is neither candy nor a sweet. All the things that you've believed might make your life complete, every dream you've ever dreamed and wished that it were true, is placed inside the castle and waiting there for you. It's marvelous and wonderful. It's perfect and ideal. It's better than the best there is and has a great appeal. So, act now. Don't lose out. Get it for a steal. For, if you buy today, my friend, I'll give you quite a deal."

"A *deal?*" asked Weebundle. "You mean… you'd make one for me?"

"And I'll throw in a slide as well," said Veigle.

"And the *whole* thing would be made out of candy?" asked Weebundle.

"Yes," said Veigle, "from the ceiling to the floor. But, alas, as much as I wish I could, I can't give my castles away for free. But, since we're such friends, and since we're so close, I'll build you a candy castle for a price lower than any price I've ever priced. I tell you what…" He pointed toward Weebundle's wagon. "I'll build you a candy castle, a castle of your very own, the best one I've ever built—if you give me some jars of preserves."

Weebundle looked at his wagon and then back at Veigle. "But I can't give you those," he said. "We need those to get through the winter. Granny Mum would be very sad if I came home without them."

"Not those jars," said Veigle. "Those are hardly enough to build the roof. I'll need your wagon stacked six rows high with those jars if you want one of my candy castles."

"Six?" asked Weebundle, stuttering the word as he said it.

"Okay," said Veigle. "Five, and that's my final offer."

"But, we barely had enough to trade for these," said Weebundle, pointing toward his wagon. "And winter's coming. We need everything we have."

Veigle gave Weebundle a look that dripped with both sincerity and compassion. Then he said, "I'm sure there must be a few things on your farm you don't need, something that's been pushed back in a cupboard, perhaps… or under a bed."

Weebundle thought about it. "We might," he said, "but I don't think anyone would trade for them, at least not enough to stack my wagon five rows high—or even one row for that matter."

"Just leave that part to me," said Veigle. "Go. Gather what you can. Then come back here, and I'll take care of the rest." With that, he stood up, clapped his hands together, and said, "Just think of it, everything you've ever wanted, everything you've ever dreamed, everything your heart desires will be waiting for you inside a delicious candy castle."

"Everything?" asked Weebundle.

"Everything," said Veigle.

Weebundle thought it over, and then he said, "Well, I guess there might be a few things we won't need. I'll ask Granny Mum. She'd know better than me."

"No!" said Veigle quickly, and then he coughed a few times. "Ummm… I think it would be best to keep it a surprise. Imagine how excited she'll be when she finds out that you're moving her from that tiny, little farm into a giant candy castle."

Weebundle imagined the look that Granny Mum would give him after she discovered they were moving into a candy castle. It made him smile. She would love it; he just knew she would. "Okay," he said finally, "I won't tell her."

"Good," said Veigle. "Now go back to your farm and gather what you can. Then come back here, to this spot, tomorrow morning. But before you go, one more peach if you please, to make our deal complete."

Weebundle opened the jar of preserves and gave Veigle another peach. After Veigle sucked it down, Weebundle waved him goodbye as he headed back to the farm.

That night, as Granny Mum sat next to the fireplace knitting a woolen sweater, Weebundle snuck out to the barn. Once he was there, he looked through the cabinets, searched every shelf, and eventually found enough items to fill his wagon. None of what he found seemed like it would be worth anything to anyone, but he did the best he could. Later that night, while he slept, his dreams were filled with candy castles. As he dreamed, the cold of winter drew nearer outside.

That morning, after Weebundle ate his breakfast and finished his chores, he told Granny Mum that he was going out to the woods. She told him to be careful and to wear his woolen sweater. He sighed as she pulled the sweater over his head. Then he gave her a hug and set off through the forest with his wagon.

When Weebundle reached his secret place, he found Veigle standing on the rock in the center of the meadow looking the same as he had the day before. As Weebundle drew closer, Veigle saw the items in Weebundle's wagon and grinned.

"How marvelous," said Veigle. "I thought you said you didn't have anything."

Weebundle pulled off his woolen sweater. Then he looked at the items in his wagon: an old shoe, a badly broken clock, a rock or two, a key that fit no lock, and several other things that he hoped would not be missed. "I don't see how anyone would want this stuff," he said, wondering why Veigle seemed so happy.

Veigle began to laugh and said, "My boy, that's only because you lack imagination. With a little imagination, you'll have your candy castle by the end of the day."

"Really?" asked Weebundle.

"Of course," said Veigle. "All you need is a 'fiboozle.' Once you have that, you'll have everything you need."

"What's a 'fib-boo-selle'?" asked Weebundle, having never heard the word before.

Veigle pointed toward Weebundle's wagon. "A fiboozle," he said, "is what's going to turn that stuff of yours into six stacks of preserves—enough to get me through the winter."

"I thought you said five," said Weebundle.

"Yes," said Veigle, "I meant five." Then he jumped down from the rock and looked over the objects in Weebundle's wagon. "A fiboozle," he explained, "is like magic."

"Magic?" asked Weebundle.

"Yes," said Veigle. "It's powerful indeed. It turns something you don't want into something that you need. It's a very simple way to sell the things you've got and charge outrageous prices, even though they're not worth squat."

"How does it do that?" asked Weebundle.

"It's simple," said Veigle. "It's all in how you present it. A fiboozle is an art. It's difficult to do, but if you learn, the more you'll earn to make your dreams come true. If you're selling something that your customers would hate, use words to dress it up as if it's something truly great. Make it look exclusive. Say that its been signed. Tell them there's a shortage, and it's difficult to find. Make a 'one-time offer.' Say it's truly rare. If they think it might get sold, they'll buy it then and there. Say it makes them popular; they'll give you all they've got. Or create a panic, and they'll buy up the whole lot. Tell them there's a study, though it's not one they can see, which says that it's a miracle—four out of five doctors agree. Tell them it's good for their body; they'll pay an extravagant fee. Say it will save the environment. If toxic, say it's 'fat free.' Tell them it's freshly organic. Tell them it goes to a cause. Tell them it hides all their wrinkles and covers up all of their flaws. Say that it helps with the ladies; men are so easy to sway. Ladies love a good bargain and things that reduce what they weigh. Children would be your best market. Fiboozle their parents to pay. For humans to trust a fiboozle, you just have to know what to say."

With that, Veigle clapped his hands together and peered down at a very confused-looking Weebundle. "Well," said Veigle, "what do you think?"

Weebundle was unsure of what to think. "It sounds like I'd be lying," he said. "And Granny Mum says that I should never lie."

Veigle stared at him for a moment. Then he cocked his head back and laughed. "And she's quite right," he said. "I would never do such a thing, and I wouldn't want you to do such a thing either. It's immoral. It's repugnant. It's…"

"Dishonest?" Weebundle offered hesitantly.

"Quite," agreed Veigle, "and we don't want that. So, instead, we'll try something else." He thought for a moment. Then he reached into his satchel and pulled out some paper and twine. "Perhaps this would work," he said. "There's no need for you to lie when you can simply wrap something up and then tie it with a bow."

"But why would I do that?" asked Weebundle.

"Simple." said Veigle. "Humans love packages tied with a bow. What's wrapped inside it? They just have to know. Oh, what could it be? Oh, what could it be? To find out the answer, they must pay a fee."

"But won't they be disappointed when they see what it is?" asked Weebundle.

"Of course not," said Veigle. "They're not paying for the object. They're paying for the thrill. The rush they get from opening it is stronger than a pill. They're paying for the experience; you're charging for the fun. And so I ask, 'Who's been harmed?' I'll tell you who, not one."

Weebundle thought it over for a moment. "I guess it's okay," he said.

"Of course it is," said Veigle. "But I suggest you tell them to wait at least six hours to open it."

"Why?" asked Weebundle.

"To make it more exciting," said Veigle. "But the one thing you must do, the one thing you must know, for them to really want it, you must put on a show. Be as cute as a kitten. Don't look afraid or distraught. Your customers have to be smitten. Charm them with all that you've got. Tell them it's fun and exciting; it might send a chill up their spine. It's something they'll always remember, so give them no room to decline. Tug at their heartstrings and smile, acting sincere and not blue, because what it is you'll be selling is not just the present—it's you."

"Me?" asked Weebundle.

"Yes," said Veigle. "Now, let's start wrapping. There's only so much daylight in a day." Then he grabbed an old shoe from the wagon and began wrapping it.

Weebundle looked at the pile of stuff in the wagon and then back at Veigle. "Are you sure this is okay?" he asked.

"Yes," said Veigle, "or we wouldn't be doing it."

"Okay," said Weebundle. Then he sat down next to Veigle and began wrapping a broken toy.

After they finished wrapping everything, they loaded the wagon and Weebundle set off toward town.

"Remember," yelled Veigle after him. "Cute as a kitten!"

"I will," said Weebundle. Then he skipped off toward the town of Hidden Hollow, while imagining how happy he and Granny Mum would be in their brand new candy castle.

When Weebundle reached town, everyone was still busy getting ready for winter, and the air was so cold that Weebundle could see his breath. Reluctantly, he reached into his wagon and pulled out his woolen sweater. He put it on. It itched, but he was too excited to care, so excited that he began rushing through the crowd. He reached Miss Prune's shop, knocked on the door, and a moment later she peered out from inside. She didn't see him at first, and Weebundle had to cough a few times for her to look down.

"Oh," she said with a smile. "There you are." Then she saw his wagon. "What have you got there?" she asked.

Weebundle explained to Miss Prune that his wagon was full of presents.

"How nice," she said. "You've got quite a lot of them. Who are they for?"

"They're for you," said Weebundle. "I want to trade them for your preserves."

Miss Prune grinned. "I would love to," she said, "but I can't trade my preserves for presents. I still need supplies for the winter, and I need them for trading."

Weebundle frowned, but then remembered what Veigle had told him. So, cute as a kitten, he looked up at her and said, "But Miss Prune, everyone needs a present. Think of how wonderful it would be to open one. It would be fun and exciting. It might send a chill up your spine. It's something you'll always remember." And he gave her no room to decline.

"That does sound exciting," said Miss Prune, "very exciting indeed. How many jars do you want?"

"I'll give you all of these presents for enough jars to fill my wagon five rows high," said Weebundle.

Miss Prune shook her head and said, "If I gave you that much, then I wouldn't have any left. I'll tell you what—I'll give you one jar of my preserves for one of your presents. How's that?"

Weebundle almost frowned again but tried to keep smiling. He couldn't go back to Veigle with only one jar, but Miss Prune was right. If he took them all, she would have nothing left to trade. Then he had a thought. "What if I got you everything you need?" he asked her. "Then would you give them to me?"

"I guess so," said Miss Prune. "But there's still a lot of things I need. I don't see how…"

"It's a deal," said Weebundle, giving her no to time to finish. Then he asked her to write down a list of all the things she would need for the winter. After she gave him the list, he gave her a present and remembered to tell her that she should wait before opening it.

"Why?" she asked, curiously.

"Because," said Weebundle, repeating what Veigle had said, "it makes it more exciting."

Mrs. Prune considered this. "I guess you're right," she said. "That would make it more exciting." Then she gave him a jar of her preserves and waved as he went on his way.

Weebundle looked at Miss Prune's list as he walked through town. There were quite a few items on it, and he hoped he had enough presents to trade for them all. His first stop was Miss Wick's candle shop. Miss Wick loved the idea of opening a present and agreed to trade five candles for one of them. Unfortunately, when Weebundle left, Mrs. Wick had to raise her prices to cover the cost of what she gave to Weebundle. The second person he visited was Mr. Chop, who thought that opening a present sounded like a wonderful idea. He traded Weebundle a stack of wood for five presents, one present for each member of his family. Though, after Weebundle left, Mr. Chop also had to raise his prices to cover the cost of what he gave to Weebundle. The third person on the list wanted three presents. The fourth person wanted four. But they each had to raise their prices for everything left in their store.

Weebundle went from shop to shop and managed to get everything on Miss Prune's list. Then he brought it all back to Miss Prune, who clapped with delight when she saw him.

"I can't believe it," said Miss Prune. "That's *more* than enough to help me get through the winter." She thanked him over and over again as she helped him unload his wagon. Then they stacked five rows of her preserves, one on top of the other, securing them with string for the journey through the forest. She also gave him an extra jar for saving her the trouble of having to trade them herself.

As Weebundle waved her farewell and headed up the hill toward his secret meadow, he failed to hear the bickering that began to erupt in the town behind him. Several people began complaining that all of the prices had soared, and the things that they needed for winter were things that they couldn't afford. So, everyone raised all their prices, and then they raised them some more, until no one could trade for the winter and panic broke out in each store. They fought, they yelled, and they argued, demanding that it wasn't right. The town then fell out of balance, as Weebundle walked out of sight.

While making his way up the path, Weebundle was completely unaware of the chaos he had left behind. Instead, he was lost in thoughts of lemon bricks, of candy sticks, and of all his dreams coming true. Unable to contain his excitement, he skipped along the path while wondering how long it would take for Veigle to build the castle. Then, as he reached the meadow, he was surprised by what he saw. He stood there with his jaw dropped and his eyes wide with wonder. The candy castle had already been built.

"Welcome back," said Veigle. Then he gestured toward the castle. "How do you like it?"

It was the most amazing sight Weebundle had ever seen, and he said so.

"Thank you," said Veigle, as he bowed. "Now, if you'll just hand over what's in your wagon, I'll give you this." He reached into his pocket, pulled out something small, and held it up in front of him.

"What's that?" asked Weebundle.

"Why, it's the key to your castle, of course," said Veigle. "You can't get in without a key." He stretched out the word *key* as he said it.

Beaming, Weebundle rolled his wagon up to Veigle and handed him the handle. "Here," said Weebundle. "But remember I warned you; they really don't taste very good. Some do, but most taste like slime. Granny Mum even says so."

"My dear child," said Veigle, "I'm not interested in how they taste."

"You're not?" asked Weebundle.

"Of course not," said Veigle. Then he began circling one of his long, boney fingers over a jar of preserves. As he did, the peaches began to disappear, and a blue mist filled the jar. "You see," he continued, "there's more in these jars than peaches and plums, oh yes. You humans have an essence, an energy. It's what gives you life, and you pass some of your energy to others in the things that you create. There's a balance in this exchange, as long as you give equal to what you take."

As he spoke, the jar of preserves began to look more like a

blue lantern, which illuminated a dark edge in Veigle's smile. "But I'm not too fond of giving," he continued, "at least not as much as I take. My castles may seem extraordinary, but they're simple and easy to make. That allows me to give you less, so there is more for me to take." Then Veigle opened the jar, raised it up to his mouth, and slowly inhaled the mist through his puckered lips. When the jar was empty, he tossed it over his shoulder, while smacking his gums together. "Dee-lish-ousss," he said, and then he began circling his finger around another jar. "Usually winters make it difficult for me to feed, but you, my dear boy, brought me all that I'll need. The energy of humans is sweeter than sweets. Thank you, oh thank you, for all of these treats."

"I don't understand," said Weebundle.

"It's not that difficult to grasp," said Veigle. "I'm a Trickster, by type and by trade. I'm sure your Granny Mum told you about us."

She had, and Weebundle took a step back. "A trickster?" he asked.

"That's right," said Veigle, proudly.

Weebundle took another step back. "But she said that tricksters drain people. She said they drain them until there's nothing left. She said, they're *monsters*."

"That's a bit harsh," said Veigle, as the mist in the jar grew brighter. "After all, I'm not the one who threw that town out of balance—you are. I simply offered you a candy castle. You didn't have enough energy of your own to give me, so you got it from someone else, and you got what you wanted." He pointed toward the candy castle. "Just like I promised." Then Veigle opened the jar he was holding and sucked it dry. "Now," he said happily, as he threw the empty jar over his shoulder, "let's go look at your brand new candy castle."

Before Weebundle could back away any further, Veigle grabbed his arm and dragged him toward the candy castle's giant doors. Then Veigle inserted the key into the lock, turned it, and stepped back as the doors swung inward.

Weebundle looked inside.

The castle was empty.

"I thought you said it would be full of everything I ever dreamed of," said Weebundle, who now felt both afraid... and confused.

Veigle laughed. "My boy, that was just a fiboozle." He handed Weebundle the key, put his arm around Weebundle's shoulder, and gestured toward the emptiness inside. "Let me tell you a little something about candy castles. They may look great on the outside, but they're an illusion, and nothing more. The inside is always empty, bare from wall to floor. If humans knew the truth, they'd refuse to pay my fee. So, I give them a fiboozle, and they beg me for a key. When they can't afford it, but want it right away, they'll find somebody foolish and fiboozle *them* to pay. Sure, I might seem cruel. Yes, I lie and cheat, but it's what tricksters do—and hey, I've got to eat."

Then Veigle patted Weebundle on the shoulder, turned around, and began walking toward Weebundle's wagon. "And," he continued, "children are the most foolish; they're trusting, as you ought to know. They believe all the things that I tell them. Their minds are like putty and dough. They don't understand a fiboozle, and take what I say as just so. I hope you enjoy your new castle, and now I'm afraid I must go."

"But that's not fair," said Weebundle. "I don't want the castle anymore. It's not what I thought it would be."

"It never is," said Veigle, "but that's not my problem. We made an agreement, and I gave you what you wanted."

"But this isn't what I wanted," said Weebundle.

"Sorry, kid, no refunds. All sales are final." With that, Veigle reached down and grabbed the wagon's handle. Then he began pulling it into the forest, just as a voice shouted out from the edge of the meadow.

"Stop right there!" yelled the voice.

Weebundle turned around and was surprised to see someone walking through the meadow. "Granny Mum?" he yelled.

It *was* Granny Mum, and the look on her face would have frozen a lake on a hot summer day, though the look was not directed at Weebundle. "I suggest," she said to Veigle, while making it clear that what she was about to say was a demand and not a suggestion, "that you run as fast as you can and leave the wagon with us."

"Madam," said Veigle, bowing as he said it. "The boy and I made a deal, and I'm simply taking what's mine. Now, if you'll excuse me, I must be on my way."

"I thought you would say that," she said. "You can't say I didn't warn you." Then she reached into her apron pocket, pulled out a fistful of salt, and threw it at him.

Veigle let out a horrible cry as it landed on him. "Madam, stop that at once!" he yelled, as he tried to brush it off. "You'll burn off my flesh!"

"I'd say that's getting off easy," she said, and then she threw another fistful of salt at him. "I mean really, taking advantage of a little one. Despicable. Now be off with you!" she yelled—and threw more salt.

Veigle screamed and cursed as the salt burnt his skin. "But we made a deal!" he demanded.

"And now I'm making a new one," said Granny Mum. "Leave the wagon and run away. If you don't, you can stay and be buried in a pile of salt." Then she drew her arm back and threw even more salt at him.

With his skin starting to blister, Veigle cursed them both and ran from the meadow as quickly as he could.

"And don't come back!" yelled Granny Mum. "I've got plenty of more salt where that came from." Then she looked down at Weebundle, who was looking up at her with a mix of confusion and relief. She smiled and patted him on the head. "You have to watch out for those Tricksters," she said. "They're always out in the forest before winter: greedy, devious, deceitful little things. I should have made him eat the salt. That would have taught him a lesson."

Weebundle was still trying to understand everything that had just happened. "How did you know I was here?" he asked.

"Well," she said. "I had an interesting visit from Mr. Chop, then Miss Wick, and then a few other people from town. They weren't very happy, and I dare say, they had good reason not to be."

Weebundle looked down at the ground, feeling ashamed for what he had done.

Granny Mum chuckled, and she patted Weebundle on the head again. "Don't worry yourself about it," she said. "After they came, I figured you must have gotten caught up with a trickster. So, I got some salt and came looking for you. They hate salt. Though, I will say, if it wasn't for this giant candy thing, I don't think I would have ever found you."

"I'm sorry," said Weebundle. "I just wanted to live in a candy castle... with you."

"Is that what this is?" she asked, looking up at the candy castle. "That was very thoughtful of you, but I'm quite happy where I am. I don't need a castle. I just need you."

Weebundle looked up at her, almost afraid to meet her eyes. He had never done anything like this before. "Are you mad at me?" he asked.

"Of course not," she said, "why would I be? You were tricked. Happens to the best of us, old and young. What's important is not what you did; what's important is what you learned from it. Plus, you taught everyone else in that town a bit of a lesson. And if they're mad at you, then that's their problem."

"But I don't want them to be mad at me," said Weebundle. "Is there anything I can do?"

"The first thing we can do," she said, "is bring these jars back. That should put everything back in balance. Everyone needs Miss Prune's preserves in order to get through the winter." Then she chuckled and said, "No matter how bad they may taste." She grabbed the wagon's handle with one hand and Weebundle's hand with the other. "Come along," she said. "We haven't much light left, and there is much to undo."

"But, what about the candy castle?" asked Weebundle.

"Best to leave it be," said Granny Mum.

And *leave it be*, they did. Then, they headed back to town where apologies were accepted, lessons were learned, feelings were mended, and the balance returned.

As the last leaf of autumn descended and flurries filled the air, the townsfolk greeted the winter, forgetting the castle was there. As snow blankets covered the forest, the castle began to break

down. The peppermint columns fell over; the floors melted down to the ground. The walls dissolved into puddles, the chimneys collapsed into heaps, and nothing was left but the meadow, no fruit-flavored candies or sweets. Soon flowers would bloom with the springtime, a wonderful treat for the bees. The animals would wake from their slumber, and the birds would fly back to their trees. There's a balance to life and to living. This balance affects one and all. Each thing that you do makes a difference, no matter how big or how small. So, always be careful of Tricksters while making your path through the woods. And always wear your wool sweater, when Granny Mum says that you should.

———————.

What a pleasant ending. Things turned out for the best. The next one is an epic that starts off with a quest. There's someone searching high and low in every tree and mound. Let us keep on reading, and we'll find out what they found.

DOODLES, GLIXIES, AND A GIANT THUMPIN

"How did I get here?" thought Dillip. It was a question he tried to answer as he crouched behind a rock and anxiously awaited the giant Thumpin. Doodles and Glixies were already gathering on opposite sides of the meadow. As Dillip watched them prepare to battle each other, he feared the worst and hoped that the giant Thumpin would arrive before someone got hurt. While the Doodles and the Glixies sharpened sticks and gathered rocks, Dillip remembered how the whole thing—the girl, the war, and the giant Thumpin—began with a question, a quest, and a moment he'd never forget.

Dillip was a Doodle, and Doodles were tiny creatures that grew to about a foot in height. They had short, floppy ears and long, bushy tails. They were peaceful and known for their sunflower cakes, their raspberry juice, and their outbursts of spontaneous "yadels," a burst of thought that sprang from the heart of a Doodle.

Dillip was born the son of Digger, the leader of a tribe of Doodles living in a patch of sunflowers on the edge of a cliff. The cliff overlooked a darkened lake nestled deep in the center of a dense mountain forest. Dillip was young, and unlike the other Doodles, he had never recited a yadel. That was because Dillip thought he had nothing profound to say, since he had never gone anywhere or done

anything worth yadeling about. His father was the adventurer, and Dillip was the son who stayed home. That changed the day his father passed away and Dillip became the leader of their tribe.

Dillip loved his tribe and wanted to be a good leader, but he wasn't sure what a leader did. So, he asked his advisors, and they told him that a leader's job was to unite the tribe. When their tribe had trouble surviving in nature, a leader united them by building their village. When their tribe had trouble finding food, a leader united them by building windmills to grind sunflower seeds into powder. When their tribe had trouble finding water, a leader united them by building a bucket and pulley system that collected water from the lake at the bottom of the cliff. His advisors then explained that, once their tribe had food, water, and shelter, each leader that followed would unite the tribe by reciting yadels.

The thought of having to recite a yadel made Dillip feel uneasy, since he still felt like he had nothing to say. So, he decided to do something he never thought he would do. He climbed down the cliff, stood on the edge of the lake, and summoned The Great Aponottle.

The Great Aponottle was an exceptionally old, remarkably wise, and some would say, "incredibly frightening," creature that lived at the bottom of the lake. Those who had questions would summon it for answers. The only way to summon The Great Aponottle was to throw rocks into the lake, with the hope of hitting it on the head. As Dillip gathered rocks and threw them into the lake, he couldn't help but feel a little anxious and frightened. While he had never seen The Great Aponottle, he had heard that it could be terribly cranky, which he guessed would be an appropriate response to being hit on the head with a bunch of rocks.

After Dillip threw his rocks, he waited, but nothing happened. Just as he was about to throw in some larger rocks, bubbles began rising to the surface of the lake. Soon waves began to crash against the shore, as the monstrous shape of The Great Aponottle rose out of the water. Its tentacles glistened and its scales gleamed, as its eyes set in a glowering stare toward Dillip, who was now gripping his tail so tightly that it was turning blue. The Great Aponottle was truly a shocking sight, one that would make most creatures run in fright, but Dillip gathered his courage to do what he went there to do and ask what he came there to ask.

"Oooooh great and wise Aponottle...," he began, trying to sound more respectful than scared.

The Great Aponottle rolled its eyes and sighed. Then, with a deep and *annoyed* voice, it said, "Would you mind skipping the flattering bit and just ask your question? The sooner you ask it, the sooner I can answer it. Then I can start nursing this headache you've given me—thank you very much."

"Oh," said Dillip, "okay, sorry. Well, I was hoping you might know a good way for a leader to unite a tribe."

"I see," said The Great Aponottle. It thought for a moment. Then it cleared its enormous throat and said, "It's simple. All you need is an *adversary*."

"What's an 'ad-ver-sary?'" asked Dillip, having never heard the word.

"It's something your tribe can unite against that will keep it united as long as you have one. There, your question has been answered. Now go away." With that, The Great Aponottle began sinking back into the lake.

"Wait," said Dillip. "I still don't understand what an 'ad-ver-sary' is."

The Great Aponottle sighed a deeper sigh and said, "If I tell you, will you leave?"

"Yes," said Dillip, who was as ready to leave as The Great Aponottle was to get rid of him.

"Fine," said The Great Aponottle. Then it dove back down into the lake. A moment later it resurfaced, holding a tiny, thin tablet. It cleared its throat, looked down at the tablet, and read what it said to Dillip. "An adversary," it began, "is a rebel or a foe, an enemy or rival that disrupts the status quo—an opponent or invader, malicious through and through, disputing what you think and opposing what you do. If you get one, it will boost your patriotic pride. It strengthens commonality, puts differences aside. It raises self-esteem, eases worry and distress, by distracting you with what they think, how they talk, or dress. By rejecting how they live, their beliefs and point of view, an adversary can be used to bind your tribe like glue."

The eyes of The Great Aponottle looked up from the tablet and then down at Dillip. "There," it said, "that should explain it. Instructions are at the bottom. Good luck." Then it gave the tablet to Dillip and dove back down into the lake.

As the lake became calm again, Dillip found himself still unsure of what to do. So, he decided to drag the tablet back to his village and ask his advisors.

Dillip had two advisors. Advisor One was named Pound. He was old and round. Advisor Two was named Prim. She was old and thin. Together they helped Dillip with difficult decisions, and so Dillip read to them what The Great Aponottle had read to him. Afterward, he asked them what they thought.

"It certainly sounds interesting," said Pound.

"I like the idea," said Prim. "But I think it would be easier if you just recited a yadel. It's always worked in the past."

"I know," said Dillip, "but my heart still has nothing to say. I've tried, but nothing's there."

"Well then," said Prim, "perhaps an ad-ver-sary *is* a good idea."

"But, how would we get one?" asked Pound.

Dillip looked down at the instructions near the bottom of the tablet. "It says here that we need to find another village—a village that's different than ours."

"What do we do once we've found it?" asked Pound.

"Apparently," said Dillip, "we unite our village by trying to change their village to be more like ours."

"That sounds easy enough," said Prim. Pound nodded in agreement, as Dillip tried to make out a warning written at the bottom of the tablet. Unfortunately, most of the warning was gone, having broken off when Dillip struggled to drag the tablet up the side of the cliff. Hoping the warning wasn't important, Dillip decided that he and his advisors would set out the following morning and unite their tribe by finding an adversary.

The next morning, the tribe of Doodles whistled, cheered, and recited yadels, as Dillip and his advisors set off through the forest. They walked all morning until they came across a giant "Happagood" tree. Every creature in the forest knew that Happagood trees were usually inhabited by "Friendlies." A Friendlie was a furry creature and slightly smaller than a Doodle. It had a head like a chipmunk, feet like a rabbit, and claws like a cat. It also had a long, thin tail. Its fur was green, except for its ears which were black.

As Dillip and his advisors drew closer to the Happagood tree, they saw some Friendlies hopping through its branches. They were gathering nuts and flowers, singing to each other as they did. The tune they sang was catchy, much like the flu, in that it made the Doodles feel sick after hearing it.

"We're so happy, la le le. Happy, happy, in our tree. Join me for a cup of tea. Happy, sappy, flappy, wee…" and so on.

As the Doodles covered their ears, the Friendlies began hopping back to their village near the top of the tree. When the Friendlies were gone, Dillip asked his advisors if they thought the Friendlies would make good adversaries. They believed the Friendlies certainly looked different and sounded different, but their village sat pretty high off the ground, and none of the Doodles wanted to hear them sing again. So, they decided to move on.

As the morning turned into afternoon, they came across a small, moss-covered cave. Venturing inside, Dillip and his advisors found a village of "Glowdows." A Glowdow was slightly taller than a Doodle. It had ears like a bat, a nose like a possum, and the tips of its tail lit up like a lantern, which made living in the dark more livable.

The Glowdows were definitely different enough, but as Dillip and his advisors wondered if they had found their adversary, they heard a terrible noise erupt from the back of the cave. The Glowdows stiffened as their tails grew brighter. Moments later, Dillip and his advisors were running out of the cave, as the Glowdows were attacked by a family of raccoons who wanted the cave for themselves. Instead of staying to see who won, or what was left of who lost, Dillip and his advisors decided to move on.

The next village they found was near a waterfall, just beyond a meadow of wildflowers. The waterfall was surrounded by ferns, and under the ferns lived a tribe of "Glixies." A Glixie was similar to a Doodle, except that they had the eyes of an owl and the ears of a fox. Their tails were less bushy, and they had two tiny horns that stuck out from the top of their head. Feeling hopeful, Dillip and his advisors decided to get a closer look. As they hid behind a fern, they noticed that the village was built mostly out of driftwood. Scattered throughout the village were carts full of berries, barrels full of honey, and ferns that grew beside every door. There was also a tiny watermill and several gardens, which the Glixies were busy tending to—except for the one that walked up behind Dillip and tapped him on his shoulder.

"Who are you?" asked the Glixie, sternly.

Startled, Dillip turned around—and would remember the next moment for the rest of his life. Behind him stood a Glixie, a girl Glixie, who seemed not much older than him. He thought her hair looked like a red sunset, and her face put the beauty of flowers to shame. Her eyes looked bluer than ice. Her fur looked as brown as an acorn. Her horns reflected the light of the sun and looked about as sharp as the stick she was holding. Dillip was so overwhelmed by the sight of her that it took him a moment to realize the point of her stick was pointing at him.

"I asked you a question," said the Glixie. "Who are you?"

Dillip tried to think of an answer, but he was finding it difficult to speak. So, he looked toward his advisors for help.

"Um, madam," said Pound, who then yelped and hid behind Prim when the Glixie pointed her stick at him.

Prim rolled her eyes, kicked at Pound, and then politely said, "We're sorry to bother you, but we were passing by and wanted to ask you a few questions."

"What kind of questions?" asked the Glixie, raising an eyebrow.

"Well," said Prim, "questions like, 'What foods do you eat?'"

"What beliefs do you have?" said Pound.

"What things do you like?" said Prim.

"What thoughts do you think?" said Pound.

The Glixie looked over at Dillip, as if expecting him to give her a question as well, but all he could do was smile at her. It was a dreamy kind of smile that was then met with a smile from the Glixie, and with some curious stares from his advisers.

"Okay," said the Glixie, and she lowered her pointed stick. "That sounds harmless enough." Then she allowed Dillip's advisors to ask her their questions. Dillip tried to think of a question himself, but the Glixie kept smiling at him, which seemed to make his head feel fuzzy. Plus, his ears kept twitching and his face felt flushed. His stomach felt funny as well. He didn't know what was wrong with him. Was he getting sick? He certainly felt like he was. Before he could think of a single question, his advisors had finished and were preparing to leave.

Dillip turned to leave with them but looked back to find that the Glixie was watching him as they went. She smiled at him again, and he almost tripped. The smile seemed to have a twist to it, a sparkle, the corners of which were met by a slight blush in her cheeks.

"I'm Geela," she said to him, still smiling.

To his bewilderment, Dillip couldn't remember his name. All he could say was, "I'm... um... ugh...," which seemed to make Geela smile even wider.

"My father is the leader of our tribe," she said. "I'm sure he won't mind if you come back with more questions." Then she turned to leave but added, "I wouldn't mind either. Perhaps by then, you'll have a name." With that, she was gone, leaving Dillip with both a loss for words and some feelings he had never felt before. He realized he must have looked like he felt, because his advisors were staring at him curiously.

"Are you alright?" asked Pound.

Dillip shook his head. "I'm not sure," he said. "For some reason, I've forgotten my name."

His advisors stared at him for a moment. Then they both shrugged their shoulders and began going over Geela's answers as the three of them made their way home.

"They certainly look different," said Pound.

"And they act different," said Prim.

"And they think different," said Pound.

"She was definitely different," said Dillip.

"I think the Glixies would make perfect adversaries," said Prim.

"As do I," said Pound. "Do you agree?" he asked Dillip.

Dillip was still having trouble thinking. Staring at Geela had been like staring at the sun. She had left an impression that blinded him to any other thought but her. "I seem to be having an issue with my head," he said, finally.

"Don't worry about that," said Prim. "Most of us do. And, if I may say, by making the Glixies our adversaries, we might find ourselves so distracted that we'll never have to deal with our issues again."

"Wouldn't that be nice?" asked Pound.

"Nice indeed," said Prim. "Then it's settled. The Glixies will be our adversaries. When we get back, we can unite our tribe by launching a campaign to make the Glixies more like us."

Dillip decided to agree with his advisors, and when they returned to their village, the announcement was made. Then, that very next day, the Doodle's left their village with the ambitious goal of changing the Glixies to be more like them. Of course, their goal would have been much easier to achieve if the Glixies had wanted to change, but the Glixies thought they were fine just the way they were. In fact, Geela's father found that he also needed something to unite his tribe, and having an adversary seemed like a splendid idea. So, Geela's father united the Glixies against the Doodles. And, as the Doodles tried to change the Glixies, the Glixies tried to change the Doodles. This continued throughout the spring and into the summer, since neither the Doodles nor the Glixies wanted to change.

While the Doodles and Glixies quibbled and bickered over who should change who, Dillip and Geela snuck away and spent each day together. They walked through the meadows, swam in the streams, and stared at the stars, as both of them realized that they had more in common than they had differences. Then, as often happens in situations like these, Dillip and Geela fell in love, which could explain why they were completely unaware of the war that was about to break out between their tribes.

One night, as Dillip slept soundly in his hut, he was awakened by a whisper in his ear.

"Wake up, wake up…"

Dillip slowly opened his eyes to find Geela standing over him. He guessed he was still dreaming because he had been dreaming of her. He smiled peacefully and closed his eyes again, which then shot open when she slapped him across the face.

"I need to talk to you," she said. "Now."

Dillip groaned. It was still mostly dark out, but he could see a faint glow of sunrise through his window. He rubbed his cheek as Geela sat down beside him.

"What's wrong?" he asked her, knowing it must be something bad—and it was.

Geela told him that her father had grown tired of the Doodles trying to change the Glixies, and that he had decided to declare war on the Doodles. "And there's a worse part," she said.

"There's a worse part?" He thought it sounded pretty bad already, but it got worse.

"My father won't let me see you anymore."

"What? But why? I didn't do anything."

"Are you still asleep?" She thumped him on the forehead. "You're the leader of your tribe, and my father is the leader of our tribe. He didn't want me seeing you in the first place. Now he's forbidden it."

Dillip was now wide awake. "This can't be happening."

"It is happening, and my father is planning to attack your tribe this time tomorrow."

Dillip groaned and shook his head as he imagined all the horrible things that could happen to his tribe, or Geela's tribe... or Geela. He knew there had to be something he could do, some way he could stop it. Then he had an idea. "What if I convinced my tribe to accept the Glixies the way they are? Would your father call off his attack?"

Geela thought for a moment and nodded her head. "He might," she said.

As Dillip considered this plan, he realized that only a yadel would convince his tribe to accept the Glixies, and it would have to be a good one. The thought made him cringe, since he still felt like he had nothing to say.

"What's wrong?" asked Geela, seeing the change in his expression.

"Nothing," said Dillip, who was now twisting his tail in his hands. "I...," he started, but was interrupted when Geela took his hands away from his tail.

"You'll be fine," she said gently. "I believe in you." Then she kissed him and said, "You're their leader, so lead them."

Dillip smiled a little. The kiss had helped, but her words had helped more. She was better at words than he was, but the Doodles wouldn't listen to her, even if she yadeled. Besides, it was his mess to clean up. So, before her kiss could wear off, he got out of bed, straightened himself up, and told Geela to wait for him. Then he walked out into the sunrise to gather his tribe together.

After Dillip left, Geela stood by the door and listened. At first it was difficult for her to hear anything, but then there was a loud commotion, followed by some cheering and then applause. Shortly after, Dillip returned to the hut, and Geela asked him how it went.

Dillip closed the door and tried to smile. "Well," he said, "the good news is that I know a safe way to get you out of here."

Geela stared at him for a moment and then frowned. "If that's the good news, what's the bad news?"

Before he answered her, Dillip checked his windows to make sure no one could see them. Then he said, "I told them that your father declared war on us. But, before I could say anything else, they decided to declare war on you. Then they started cheering and yadeling, and they didn't hear another word I said. I've never seen them like this before, never." At that point, he kicked at the air in frustration. "I wish I had never gone to see The Great Aponottle. This was supposed to unite my tribe, not get them all killed, or get you..."

"Wait," said Geela, interrupting him. "Are you saying The Great Aponottle told you to do this? Why?"

"I just wanted to be a good leader," he said. Then he told her about his trip to see The Great Aponottle and the advice he was given. When he finished, Geela looked angry, and he was relieved to find that it wasn't toward him.

"If The Great Aponottle told you to do this," she said, "then it should also know how to undo it, right?"

Dillip guessed she was right, and then he hoped she was right, as they left his hut, snuck past the other Doodles, and made their way down the cliff to speak with The Great Aponottle. After reaching the lake, and throwing in their rocks, The Great Aponottle rose out of the lake and let out a deep sigh when it saw Dillip.

"You again," it grumbled, as it rubbed its head.

"Oooooh Great Aponottle…," Dillip began, but was interrupted by Geela.

"'Great Aponottle,' my horns!" she yelled. Then she gave it a look that would have caused most animals to run away.

Dillip nudged Geela's side with his shoulder. "Geela," he whispered, "you're going to make it angry."

"I'm the one who's angry," said Geela. Then she pointed her finger at The Great Aponottle. "You're supposed to be all wise and knowing, but thanks to your advice, our tribes are going to war with each other."

The Great Aponottle looked down at Geela. "And, who are you?" it asked.

"I'm Geela," she said, "of the Glixie tribe, and you should be ashamed of yourself. Do you realize how much trouble your advice has caused?"

"It wasn't me," said The Great Aponottle. "I simply gave the advice. It was the Doodle who followed it. I warned him that uniting his tribe by opposing another could cause a war."

"No, you didn't," said Dillip.

"I most certainly did," said The Great Aponottle. "It was on the tablet I gave you… near the bottom. You couldn't miss it."

"Oh," said Dillip. "Well… that part kind of broke off."

Geela put her hand on her forehead and groaned. Then she returned her attention to The Great Aponottle. "Since it was your advice, do you know of any way we can undo the damage it caused?"

"There is a way," said The Great Aponottle. "For, when two tribes find themselves skirmishing as foes, find a *third* tribe to which the two tribes can oppose. With a common enemy, you'll put differences aside. By distracting with a third, two tribes become allied."

Geela frowned and rolled her eyes. "You call that advice? If we did that, then we'd have to fight another tribe."

"That is correct," said The Great Aponottle. "But it would keep you from fighting each other."

"This is ridiculous," said Geela, as her tail stiffened—a sure sign that she was getting even more angry.

Dillip saw this, and he quickly stepped in between Geela and The Great Aponottle, though he wasn't sure who he was protecting from whom. "What she means is that... Well, we'd prefer some advice that didn't involve having to fight anyone."

"I see," said The Great Aponottle. "Well, that's my advice. You can take it or leave it, as long as you leave. I have other things I'd rather be doing." With that, The Great Aponottle dove back down into the lake, leaving Dillip and Geela no closer to a resolution than when they arrived.

As the water settled and the lake became calm, Dillip stood there with Geela, unsure of what to do next. He knew if they didn't stop the war from happening, whatever happened would be his fault. It was an awful thought, but he didn't have much time to think it, because Geela suddenly clapped her hands together and said, "I've got it. I think I know how we can stop them. All we need is a distraction, something to distract our tribes from fighting each other. Then no one would get hurt... a big distraction, something so dangerous, so hideous, and so horrifying that our tribes would stop fighting and run away." She was so excited by her idea that she jumped up and down until she saw Dillip's face. He looked worried. "What's wrong?" she asked.

"You realize that means we would have to find something dangerous, hideous, and horrifying, right?"

"Right," she said happily, "and I know just the place to find it."

Then, for the rest of the morning and that afternoon, Geela led Dillip through the forest while telling him about a giant "Thumpin" that lived in an abandoned barn. Thumpins were quite dangerous and known to eat whatever came close to them, but this particular Thumpin owed Geela a favor. And she believed it would be the perfect thing to distract their tribes from fighting each other.

While Dillip shared her belief that a Thumpin would be frightening enough to scare their tribes, he also believed that seeking one out was dangerous. He had heard about Thumpins from his father. They were five times the size of a Doodle. They looked kind of like frogs, except they stood on two feet. Their arms were so long that their hands drug along the ground behind them. Worst of all, were their sharp, jagged teeth that always looked as if they just finished eating something. Needless to say, Dillip felt a bit apprehensive as Geela led him toward something that had played an active role in his childhood nightmares.

The sun was setting by the time Dillip and Geela reached the Thumpin. The barn in which the Thumpin lived had been abandoned by humans long ago. Its frame was rotted. Moss covered most of its walls, and the dark shadows of dusk covered the rest of it. There were fireflies drifting through the air around it, and to Dillip's horror, a long, green tongue kept shooting out through the broken windows to snatch them.

"Are you sure this is a good idea?" he asked Geela, just as the tongue shot out and snatched a bird that had flown too close to the barn.

"Don't worry," she said, squeezing his hand. "Everything will be fine."

The inside of the barn looked more frightening than the outside, mostly because it was almost too dark to see anything. A few shafts of light streamed down from cracks in the rafters, which allowed Dillip to spot something moving at the other end of the barn.

"Hello?" said Geela to the *something* at the other end of the barn.

The *something* turned around, and Dillip almost fainted. It was a Thumpin, and it was bigger and more frightening than Dillip had imagined. He thought it was definitely something to run from rather than talk to, but Geela talked to it anyway, while Dillip tried to look brave.

"I have come to ask a favor," said Geela.

As she said it, the Thumpin began lurching toward them. The floorboards creaked under its weight, and its toenails scratched against the floor with each step that it took.

"Geela…" whispered Dillip.

"It's okay," she whispered back, still standing strong and unafraid.

Dillip, who was less unafraid, whispered, "What do you think the word 'okay' means, exactly?"

The Thumpin stopped a few feet in front of them. It looked down at Dillip and then at Geela. It grunted, and then it spoke. "What is your favor?" it asked. Its monstrous voice made the hairs on Dillip's tail stand up, but Geela seemed unaffected by it. All Dillip could do was listen, as Geela explained to the Thumpin how the Doodles and the Glixies planned to battle each other at sunrise.

"And what do you want of me?" asked the Thumpin.

"We were thinking you could scare them," said Geela. "You know, before they start fighting each other. Then maybe they'll run away, and no one will get hurt."

The Thumpin squinted its eyes, as if it were trying to think. Then it asked a question neither Geela nor Dillip had thought to ask themselves. "What will keep them from fighting another day?"

Geela looked at Dillip and then back at the Thumpin. "Well…," she began, but couldn't think of anything else to say.

In the silence that followed, Dillip remembered what The Great Aponottle had told them, and he had an idea. Then he did something he never thought he would do—he spoke to a Thumpin. "What if you came by our villages every once in a while and scared everyone? If you did that, our villages would have something to focus on besides each other." Then he looked at Geela…"A common enemy, like The Great Aponottle said."

"That could work," said Geela. "Would you do that?" she asked the Thumpin.

The Thumpin thought for a moment. Then it nodded its head and said, "I will do this for you. I could even eat some of them—if you'd like. I believe *that* would frighten them."

"Yes, it would," said Geela. "But, no… You don't need to eat anyone. Just growl and stomp around a bit. That should be enough."

"Are you sure?" asked the Thumpin. "I'd only eat a few of them."

"No," said Geela, sternly this time. "Just scare them, okay? Promise?"

"Okay," said the Thumpin. "I promise. I won't eat anyone, but let me know if you change your mind."

With that, Geela and Dillip left the barn and began their journey home. As they walked beneath the stars, they talked about their plan and hoped that it would work. Dillip also hoped that the giant Thumpin would keep its promise and that no one would get hurt—or eaten.

When morning came, Dillip and Geela were crouched behind a rock watching their tribes gather at opposite ends of a meadow. Dillip's advisors recited yadels to the Doodles, while Geela's father smeared berry juice on the faces of the Glixies. Each tribe sharpened sticks and stacked up rocks as Dillip and Geela waited anxiously for the giant Thumpin. Then, all at once, there came the blowing of horns and the banging of drums as the Doodles and Glixies prepared to attack each other.

"It's too late," said Geela.

Though, just as she said it, a horrifying cry echoed through the woods. Animals fled and birds flew away as the giant Thumpin jumped out of the trees and into the meadow. Its teeth were gnashed. Its eyes glowed red. Puddles of drool dripped from its mouth. It stomped its feet. It bared its claws. It let out a terrifying howl that caused the flowers in the field to wilt with fear, and it had a similar effect on the Doodles and Glixies.

"It's working," said Dillip, and it was. Both the Doodles and the Glixies had stopped advancing on each other and found themselves too frightened to move. The Thumpin lunged at the Doodles. It growled at the Glixies. It beat on its chest with its large, scaly hands. It jumped. It spit. It even stood on its head. It did all of this over and over again until something unexpected happened.

The "something unexpected" began with a blustering cry that rose in the air and startled the Thumpin. Before the Thumpin could think, before it could run, the Doodles and the Glixies united together—and attacked it. They beat on its scales. They jumped on its back. They tripped up its feet as it snarled and spat. Then it yelped and yowled a horrible sound, as its arms and legs were bound to the ground.

After the Thumpin was secured, Geela's father took the thickest, sharpest stick he could find and climbed on top of the Thumpin's chest. He raised the stick into the air, and just as he was about to put an end to the Thumpin, Geela jumped out from behind the rock and yelled for him to stop. Startled, Geela's father turned to find his daughter and Dillip running toward him from across the meadow.

"Stop!" Geela yelled again. "You're making a mistake!"

Her father looked down at the Thumpin, then at the stick he was holding, and then back at Geela. "Really?" he asked. "I believe I'm doing it right—pointed part down and push."

Several members of each tribe nodded in agreement.

"No," said Geela, who had just reached the Thumpin. "I mean, don't kill it."

Her father looked even more confused. "Why not?" he asked.

"Because it's with us," said Dillip. Then he and Geela quickly climbed on top of the Thumpin.

"What are you doing?" asked her father. "Are you mad? It's trying to kill us."

As he said that, Dillip's advisors pushed their way through the crowd and climbed on top of the giant Thumpin.

"What do you mean it's with you?" asked Prim. The question was then repeated by Pound and then by Geela's father.

It was Geela who answered them. "We asked the Thumpin to frighten you. We thought it would keep you from fighting each other, but I didn't think you'd try to kill it."

"Neither did I," said Dillip.

"Neither did I," said the Thumpin.

"This is unacceptable," said Geela's father.

"What do we do now?" asked Prim.

"We could start fighting again," said Pound.

"You could set me free," said the Thumpin.

Then more arguing broke out across the meadow, and soon the Doodles and the Glixies were preparing to battle each other again.

Dillip knew he needed to say something, and quickly, but what should he say? Would they even listen to him? Fear began to fill his head, but then he began to wonder why he felt afraid. Hadn't he faced The Great Aponottle? Hadn't he talked to a giant Thumpin? Hadn't he fallen in love? He had gone so many places and learned so many things. The most important thing he'd learned was from Geela, who had taught him that we need differences to show us how unique we are. We need differences to mirror the things we might want to change within ourselves. We need differences to keep us from thinking there is only one path to follow. As Dillip thought about this, something began to stir in his heart, and words began to form in his head. In that moment, Dillip realized that he was no longer a Doodle who had nothing to say. So, he raised his hands, stood proudly on top of the giant Thumpin, and yelled, "Everyone! Everyone, please! I have something I want to say!"

It took a moment for his words to echo across the meadow. As each Doodle heard them, they immediately stopped what they were doing. They put down their rocks, lowered their sticks, and became silent, as each of them turned to look up at Dillip. The Glixies didn't know what was happening, so they looked up at Dillip as well. Even the Thumpin was quiet. Dillip's advisors, who had been arguing with Geela's father, were now staring at Dillip with stunned looks on their faces, realizing that he was about to give his very first yadel. Then, with the attention of the entire meadow, he began:

"I often found, while musing,
That life can be confusing.
What road should I be using?
Which path should I be choosing?
For answers I kept digging,
And soon my head was fizzing
With thoughts of ways for living,
Which now to you I'm giving.
Be accepting, not rejecting,
And spend your lives respecting.
Use words that aren't dejecting,
And to others, be protecting.
Be helpful, kind, and loving,
No pushing and no shoving.
Be truthful, never bluffing,
And feed those who have nothing.
Be genuine, not mocking.
Use empathy while talking.
Greet others while you're walking,
And look both ways while crossing.
Be friendly, not abusing,
Forgiving, not accusing,
Loving, never bruising,
...And that's what I've been musing."

As the last word was spoken, Dillip turned around and saw that Geela was smiling at him. It was the same smile she had given him on the first day they'd met. His heart filled with words, as he walked across the Thumpin, took her hands in his, and said:

"And I must say there's nothing
Like when my heart is gushing.
My head is dazed and rushing
With love that leaves me blushing.
I'm whirling and I'm reeling
With every glance I'm stealing,
And I can't bear concealing
The feelings that I am feeling.
I stand here now declaring,
As in your eyes I'm staring,
With you I vow on sharing
A love beyond comparing."

When he finished, Geela looked at him and said, "I might not be able to say it like you, but I can say that in all the times I dreamed of love, I never dreamed it would feel as good as it feels with you."

Then, as they stood on top of the giant Thumpin, Dillip and Geela kissed. It was a kiss that only those in love can kiss. It was a kiss that touched the hearts of all who witnessed it, and it would be remembered in many yadels to come.

As applause broke out through the meadow, Dillip's advisors congratulated him on his first yadel.

"It was amazing," said Pound.

"Beautiful," said Prim.

"Very touching," said the Thumpin.

After kissing again, Dillip and Geela drew away from each other and waved at the cheering crowd. Dillip's yadel had succeeded in convincing the Doodles to accept the Glixies, while Geela's love for Dillip had succeeded in convincing her father, and the rest of the Glixies, to accept the Doodles. It was a wonderful sight to see as the Doodles and the Glixies dropped their sticks, threw down their rocks, and came together as one. They also released the giant Thumpin, who was quite happy to be freed—and even kept its promise not to eat them.

After that day, the Doodles and the Glixies learned to appreciate each other's differences, and peace was made between the tribes. Then, as often happens in situations like these, love united the tribes together with the marriage of Dillip and Geela. As generations passed, the differences between the tribes began to fade. They became more and more alike, until there was little difference between the two, and the two became one. For several more generations, the tribe lived in peace, until one day their new leader wondered how she could bring the tribe closer together. So, she climbed down the cliff, spoke to The Great Aponottle, and the whole thing started all over again.

There's time for one last story before it's time to go. It starts off with a question that was asked some time ago. Someone tried to answer it. They gave it their best shot. Lets read on to see if they could answer it or not.

AN ANSWER FOR THE TENDLEBEES

Up on the edge of a gorge vast and deep,
Too steep to climb and too far to leap,
Lived the Tendlebees, tiny in size,
With bright white wings and big, round eyes.
Their hands were as big as their soft, furry feet.
They were kind, loving, and awfully sweet.
They all lived in peace with no thoughts in their head.
They played through the day and made oak leaves their bed.
They swam in the falls and flew through the trees.
It was a great life for the Tendlebees.

But then they all did what had never been done.
Rather than spending the day having fun,
They crossed the great gorge to see what was there
And saw some new sights as they flew through the air.
They passed some strange flowers and pink-colored trees,
Until they saw something that made them all freeze.
They each stared in awe at the thing that they found.
It was built out of stones on a clear patch of ground.
The front had a hole that was perfectly square,

And so they flew through it to see what was there.
The inside was dark. The air felt too cold.
Everything in it smelled dusty and old.
It looked like a cave with a floor made from trees.
It was a strange sight for the Tendlebees.

They found some odd objects and trinkets galore,
But most seemed too heavy to lift off the floor.
Then they found one that they lifted with ease
And flew it back home through the pink-colored trees.
As it was placed on a smooth, rocky mound,
They gathered to stare at the thing that they found.
They hooted; they whistled—curiosity stirred.
For what they brought back was their very first *word*.
They'd never seen one or used one before.
They liked the idea, and so they made more:
A word for the sun, a word for the sky,
A word for each cloud and each bird that flew by.
They made up a word for each flower and tree,
And soon they had named all the things they could see.

That's when it started, or so it's been said.
Their words led to *thoughts* inside of their head.
They thought and they thought. They thought quite a lot
And wanted to share all the thoughts that they thought.
They made up a *language* and learned how to speak,
And found that their thoughts were diverse and unique.
What one thought was "big," one thought was "small."

What one thought was "short," one thought was "tall."
Who's thought was wrong? Who's thought was right?
This led them to argue and use words to fight.

They each grew confused as their head filled with knots,
As thoughts led to questions which led to more thoughts.
They questioned the sky and why it was blue.
What was the answer? Nobody knew.
What was the moon, and what was the sun?
They found that an answer, for each, they had none.
So they used *theories* for answers they sought
And *imagined* the answers for questions they thought.
Some thought the wind was a breath blowing by,
Exhaled by some creature that lived in the sky.
Some thought their gorge was a massive footprint
Left by a giant while out for a sprint.

Beliefs were created, creating a mess;
Whose belief to believe was anyone's guess.
Things became worse, and got more severe
When someone asked, "Why are we here?"
As they thought theories, which turned to belief,
Their lives became filled up with anger and grief.
For each of them thought their belief must be right
And held their beliefs as they fought day and night.
That's when it happened, though no one knew why.
They woke without wings and no longer could fly.
Why had they lost them? They hadn't a clue.

Would they grow back? None of them knew.
As the years passed, they started to think
The unanswered question just might be the link.
Finding the answer to "Why are we here?"
Might make their beautiful wings reappear.
Generations passed; no progress was gained.
They thought and they thought, but the question remained.
They created beliefs, far too many to name.
But none of them worked, and their wings never came.
They started to think they were stuck on the ground
Until the day came when an answer was found.

———

Our story begins as a young Tendlebee named Key looked out on the start of a beautiful day. The sun was up, the mist had faded, and she could see all the way to the other side of the great gorge. She was sitting on her favorite flower, which bloomed on the surface of a tiny pond. She often sat there all day and then returned to her village when the flower closed at night. When morning came, the flower would open again, and Key would say "Hello" to the flower as if greeting a dear friend. Then she would sit gently within its bloom to stare out at the day.

As she sat there that morning, she remembered a time when she looked out at the gorge without a thought in her mind. She remembered when she would just sit there and whistle. It had been her favorite thing to do. She also liked to skip, run, and watch as the life around her blossomed and grew, waddled and flew, and it always seemed peaceful, inviting, and new.

But that was not now. Now she was too busy thinking her thoughts to take notice of the world around her. She wished she could go back to the time when there wasn't a thought in her mind, but there was an answer to a question she needed to find.

"*The answer*," she thought to herself and shook her head, still having no idea what it could be. She'd lost track of how many days she had questioned it, and the answer seemed to get further away with each thought she thought. She had been told that finding the answer would be difficult, and it was. From the day she was asked the question, she actually believed she might find the answer and that the Tendlebees would get back their wings. Now she wasn't so sure. It seemed like such a big question for someone her age—at least she thought so—for it had only been a few seasons after she was born that a Tendlebee called Tutor had come to collect her.

Key remembered she had been sitting in a tree that day. She was sitting in the tree because her back kept tingling, possibly a fever, maybe a rash. She didn't know, but she found that rubbing against a tree had helped. As she rubbed her back against the tree, she became startled by an elderly-sounding voice.

"Come down from that tree, child," said the elderly voice.

Key looked down and found an old, grey-bearded Tendlebee standing near the base of the tree. "Who are you?" she asked him, wondering if she was in trouble for something.

"You may call me Tutor," he told her. "Now, come with me. You have much to learn."

Key sighed and then slowly climbed down from the tree. She had heard of the Tutors. They were teachers, and they taught all of the things that every young Tendlebee needed to know. Key felt like she already knew enough and would rather spend her day watching leaves fall from the trees. But there was no avoiding the Tutors, for a Tendlebee had to be taught, whether the Tendlebee wanted to be taught or not.

As Key followed Tutor through the woods, she couldn't help but giggle to herself, since Tutor's beard was so long that he kept tripping over it. Plus, the flower he wore as a hat attracted butterflies, and he had to keep waving them away with his cane.

"Tutor?" she asked, as she tried to keep up. "What are you planning to teach me?"

Tutor smiled and said, "More than you need to know, but still not enough."

Before she could ask him what he meant, they came to a patch of flowers with three other young Tendlebees sitting in the center of it.

Tutor tapped his cane on a rock to get their attention and said, "Students, this is Key." Then he pointed his cane toward each of the other Tendlebees. "This is Blink, this is Yep, and this is Twig."

Blink, Yep, and Twig waved at Key, and she waved back. Key thought they seemed nice, and they soon would become the best of friends. Blink was a round boy, rounder than most. He looked half as as wide as he was tall and seemed to wobble a little as he sat. Yep was a small girl, smaller than most. She liked playing with bugs, and she was busy petting a ladybug that was sitting on her lap. Twig was a shy boy, shyer than most. No one had ever heard him talk, but he often made strange noises while wiggling his tail.

After wishing each of them a good morning, Key sat next to

Yep and waited to hear what Tutor had to say next.

Tutor sat in front of them on a toadstool as he waved some butterflies away from his hat. Then he clapped his hands together and cleared his throat. "Today is your first day of lessons," he said, "and I have much to teach you."

"Like what?" asked Blink.

"Well," said Tutor, "first we'll start with some words. There are many to learn, like *butterfly, buttercup, beetle,* and *fern.*"

"I already know those words," Yep said proudly.

The rest of them nodded that they knew them as well.

Tutor raised an eyebrow, smirked, and then said, "Wonderful! Then we'll start with harder words instead. There's *discord, disaster, deception,* and *stress*—plus *misled, mistaken, mournful,* and *mess.*"

The four of them looked at Tutor blankly.

"I don't know any of those words," said Key.

Tutor grinned, laughed a little, and said, "Well little one, you don't learn words like that by sitting in a tree. They each have a meaning, so listen to me. *Discord* happens when we don't agree with how others think or how others see. *Disaster* is when we start to fight over whose thought is wrong and whose thought is right. *Deception* is when a thought is untrue, though what's true to others may not be to you. *Stress* comes from thoughts that can burden your head and make you all wish that you'd just stayed in bed."

Blink sighed. "These are harder than *beetle* and *fern,*" he said.

Tutor nodded. "And they get harder," he said. Then he continued their lesson by defining *misled.* "It describes a wrong turn that you take from a thought; it leaves you confused and often distraught. *Mistaken* can happen when you've found your way, but really you're walking in circles all day. *Mournful* occurs when your thoughts give up hope, you can't find the answer, and you start to mope. *Mess* is what happens when you fail to see, just what the answer could possibly be."

Blink, Yep, Twig, and Key hadn't understood most of what Tutor said, and they told him so.

"It will make sense in time," said Tutor, "but first you must learn more words. So, pay attention to what I say." Then he taught them more words through the rest of the day.

That night, while Key lay on her oak leaf, fireflies flew above her head as she stared up at the stars and thought about all the new words she had learned. They were strange words, and unlike any words she had heard before. She was used to naming things like *lilies, lilacs,* and *cricket wings,* which always made her smile. The new words didn't make her smile at all and seemed to create unhappy thoughts in her head. Normally, when she lay down in bed, she counted the stars until she fell asleep. That night, her head was so full of thoughts that it kept her up. Her head had never done that before, and she found herself unable to sleep until the moon was halfway across the sky.

Each day after that, Tutor taught them new words, and each night after that, Key seemed to have trouble sleeping. This went on from winter to spring, and Key was so busy learning new words that she barely had time to whistle or play. Then the day came when she was taught how to think, and after that day, she spent most her time in a state of dismay.

"Today," said Tutor as he sat on his toadstool, "I will teach you how to *think*."

Yep gave Tutor a puzzled look. "But I think I know how to think," she said.

"I think I do too," said Key.

"Me too," said Blink.

Twig nodded and made a strange hooting sound.

"You only think you do," said Tutor. "Now I'm going to teach you how to think a thought through. Thoughts can be simple, but some are complex, like thinking what's past and what's coming next. A long time ago, how long we forgot, a Tendlebee thought an interesting thought. She asked what could come with the following day, but what was the answer she just couldn't say. Would there be sun? Would there be rain? A dozen more questions then filled up her brain. What could happen the day after that—or the day after that day—and each day after that? Before she knew it, she thought something new. We call it the *future*. I'll teach it to you. *Tomorrow* is something that doesn't exist. It must be created, like making a list. You make this list inside of your head, by thinking of something that could lie ahead. Believing in what your tomorrow could bring, makes it as real as the flowers in spring."

Key raised her hand. "Are you saying that I can create a *tomorrow* in my head, and the *tomorrow* will happen?"

"Well," said Tutor, "just because you think your *tomorrow* will happen, doesn't mean it will. You just think it will, which makes it real. Understand?"

"I think so," said Key, though she didn't think she did. And by the look of the others, they didn't either.

"Okay," continued Tutor, "here's where it gets tough. As we filled our *tomorrow* with stuff, we figured there's something behind us too. We call it a *yesterday*. I'll teach it to you. Think of what's happened before today. Had it been sunny or had it been grey? What happened before that, and then before that, or the day before that day, and the day before that? Think backward, then forward, and soon you will find—a timeline of life has formed in your mind. You use your timeline to think where you've been, and then where you're going... how, where, and when. Got it?"

Key, Yep, and Blink looked up at Tutor, more confused than before. Twig just twiddled his fingers and hooted some more.

"So," said Key, "tomorrow is what happens after today?"

"Yes," said Tutor.

"And yesterday is what happened before today?" asked Yep.

"It is," said Tutor. "And if you put yesterday, today, and tomorrow together, you get the past, present, and future. Since we can't see, hear, or touch the past or the future, we have to think about them instead. Only by thinking about them, can you have a timeline in your head. Otherwise, it disappears. Got it?"

"Maybe," said Key, though she doubted she did as she said it.

"Wonderful," said Tutor. Then he spent the rest of the spring teaching his students how to create a past and a future, plus some new words like *remorse, regret, guilt,* and *dread.* With no time to play and no time for fun, the students sat learning till each day was done. Then, after they learned all the things they should know, they learned of the question once asked long ago.

It had been on another beautiful day that Key, Blink, Yep, and Twig sat together under the flowers while Tutor brushed a few butterflies away from his hat. Tutor seemed sad that day, at least to Key, and she asked him what was wrong.

"Well, little one," he said softly, "the day has finally come when I must teach you what every Tendlebee must be taught, the question to an answer that each Tendlebee has sought."

Tutor adjusted his seat, adjusted his hat, and then told them the story of how the Tendlebees had lost their wings. Key had never heard the story before and asked the Tutor, why. Tutor explained to Key and the rest of the class that the story is kept from each Tendlebee until they have the tools they need to answer the question of, "Why are we here?"

"But why ask us?" asked Blink. "Why not ask someone older?"

Tutor sighed. "Once we get older, we tend to get stuck in our beliefs and stop asking questions. So, we teach you words and teach you how to think. Then we teach you the question, hoping that you might think of an answer—so we can get back our wings." Then he stared at each of them as he said, "Now that you've been taught, you must understand that our future is up to you, and now it's time to use what you've learned. So, reach deep down, open your mind, and find the answer that we couldn't find."

Key, Blink, Yep, and Twig looked at each other and then back at Tutor, who seemed to be waiting for them to say something.

"You mean answer it now?" asked Key.

"Yes," said Tutor. "I was hoping it would just, you know, kind of come to you."

Key thought for a moment, as did the others. Then they thought for a few more moments, until each of them shook their head.

"I can't think of one," said Key.

"Neither can I," said Yep.

"Me either," said Blink.

Twig shrugged his shoulders and blew bubbles out of his mouth.

"Pity," said Tutor. "Then we'll meet back here in seven days. Until then, you will spend all of your time trying to think of an answer. Any answer will do, any at all. If you think of an answer, then bring it and share it with the rest of us." With that, he stood up on his toadstool, swatted at some butterflies, and wished them good luck.

Key, Blink, Yep, and Twig then went off on their own to think of the answer. Key went to the pond and sat on her flower, where she thought for the rest of day, but the answer never came. So, she thought for several more days, trying everything she was taught, and spent each day inside her mind with each thought she thought. She tried and tried again. Her thoughts went round and round. She gave it all she had, but no answer could be found.

By the next time the class met, no one had thought of an answer, and no one thought of an answer by the next class, or the class after that, or the class after that. So many classes went by without an answer that Key had lost track of them. Now, after another season had passed, Key dreaded going to class. She sat on her flower, looking out over the great gorge, remembering how wonderful her life had been before Tutor had found her scratching her back against that tree. She sighed, and then heard a familiar voice behind her.

"Key!" yelled Yep. "Hurry up. We'll be late for class!"

Key groaned. "Why do we have to hurry? We're just going to stare at each other all day."

Yep ran up to the pond and started jumping up and down obviously excited about something. "No," she said, "Blink said he thought of the answer."

Key stood up so fast that she fell over into the pond. She quickly swam to shore where Yep helped her out of the water.

"Are you sure?" asked Key, shaking herself off.

"Yes," said Yep, who started jumping up and down again.

Key whistled, then she took Yep's hand in hers, and they ran off to class. They arrived a few moments before Tutor and found Blink sitting next to Twig. Key ran up to Blink so fast that she almost knocked him over.

"Is it true?" she asked him. "Did you really think of the answer?"

"I think so," said Blink.

Before she could ask him what the answer was, Tutor arrived and climbed onto his toadstool. "Good morning," he said to them all. "So, have any of you thought of the answer?"

Blink quickly raised his hand, and Tutor almost fell over with surprise.

"That's wonderful," said Tutor, "wonderful indeed. Tell us, young Blink. What is the answer?"

Blink rolled onto his feet and told them that he had thought of the answer when he stumbled into a hole full of rabbits. "You see," he said, "the rabbits seemed happy, and all they do is eat carrots all day. So, I thought that maybe the answer to 'Why are we here?' is *to eat*."

Tutor sighed and looked disappointed. "That was a good try," he said, "though I'm afraid it's not the answer."

Blink rolled himself back to the ground as Tutor asked if anyone else had an answer.

"I might," said Yep.

Tutor cheered up a little. "Okay, Yep, what do you think the answer is?"

"Well," said Yep, "if the answer's not *to eat*, then maybe it's *to sleep*. The bears like to sleep, and the bears seem happy. So, maybe sleeping is the answer."

Tutor sighed again. "That was a good try as well, but it's still not the answer. Does anyone else have one?" he asked hopefully.

Key shook her head while Twig made some burbling sounds.

"Well then," said Tutor, "I guess we'll just sit here and think for the rest of the morning, and maybe by afternoon you'll have thought of one."

So Key, Blink, Yep, and Twig sat silently all morning trying to think of an answer, but when afternoon came, they still had no answer to give.

"Nothing?" asked Tutor.

Blink grunted and said, "My head hurts."

"Mine aches," said Yep.

"Mine feels like it's splitting," said Key.

Twig hooted, shook his head really fast, and then fell over.

"I know it's hard," said Tutor, "but you have to keep trying."

"I still think it might be *to sleep*," said Yep.

"I still think it might be *to eat*," said Blink.

"But those can't be the answer," said Tutor. "Rabbits eat and bears sleep, but why? Why are they here? Why are we here? The answer is bigger than eating or sleeping."

"Could there be more than one answer?" asked Key. "Like, we're here to eat and sleep?"

"No," said Tutor, "there's only *one* answer." Then he thought for a moment and said, "Perhaps an example would help. This is an answer that I've been working on. First, I began with where we came from. Since a bird is hatched from an egg, I think that everything around us was hatched from a giant egg by a giant bird. Then I asked, 'Why were we hatched?' When a bird is hatched from an egg, the new bird lays another egg. So, the answer to 'Why are we here?' might be that we're part of a giant bird that's about to hatch another giant egg. I told everyone my answer, but my wings didn't grow back. Then I realized there were other questions like, 'Where did the giant bird come from?' and 'Are we the egg or are we the bird?' I figure, if I can answer those questions, then maybe I can answer *the question*, and we'd get back our wings."

Key gave Tutor a confused look because she was, in fact, confused. "But that doesn't make any sense," she said. "That would be like saying we're part of a large rain drop falling from a giant cloud. Then we'd have to think of where the cloud came from and why it was raining. Then we'd have to think of what created the cloud and then what created that."

"Exactly," said Tutor. "Now you've got it."

Yep frowned. "I don't get it," she said.

"Neither do I," said Blink.

Twig shook his head, hooted, and made some gurgling sounds.

Key felt like gurgling as well. "Tutor, I don't see how we will ever answer the question. The answer could be anything."

"Exactly," said Tutor. "That's why we try to think of as many answers as possible. Eventually, one of us has to get it right."

Then Blink raised his hand. "Perhaps the bird has a giant nest."

"Or it could be in a cage," said Yep.

"Now you're thinking," said Tutor. "But only one of those could be the right answer. Which one do you think it is?"

"The nest," said Blink.

"The cage," said Yep.

Twig hooted and shrugged his shoulders.

Key looked at each of them and almost felt like screaming. Instead, she said this, "The bird could be anywhere. The egg could have come from anything—a fox, or a rainbow, or sneezed out of a giant nose."

"You're right," said Tutor. "You're exactly right. But first, we'd have to figure out why the egg was sneezed out of the giant nose."

Yep thought for a moment. "What if the giant nose had a terrible cold?" she asked.

"Good," said Tutor.

Then Blink raised his hand. "What if the giant nose was allergic to eggs?" he asked.

Tutor smiled at both Yep and Blink. "If we could answer those questions, then maybe we'd finally have our answer."

Key stood up and threw her hands into the air. "How?" she asked him. "How could that possibly give us the answer? And why would an egg be in a giant nose to begin with?"

"Maybe a giant bird laid it there," said Yep.

"Yeah," said Blink. "Maybe the giant bird thought it was a nest."

Twig crossed his eyes and fell over again.

"This is ridiculous," said Key. "Then we'd have to ask where the nose came from."

"From an egg?" asked Yep.

Key grunted to herself, looked at Tutor, and then said, "I've been thinking so hard that my head hurts. Now you want me to figure out why a giant nose sneezed out an egg that hatched into a bird— that laid an egg—that we might be inside of?"

"Exactly," said Tutor. "Answer that, and you might have the answer."

"No I won't," said Key. "I'll just have more questions."

"And you'll answer those too," said Tutor.

"But when does it stop?" asked Key.

"When the answer you answer doesn't lead to a question," said Tutor.

"But, that could take forever," said Key.

"It has," said Tutor. "For generations we've been trying to answer the question. If we don't figure it out now, then the next generation will give it a try and so will the generation after that until the question has finally been answered."

Key couldn't believe what she was hearing. She stared hopelessly at Tutor, realizing she might spend the rest of her life trying to answer a question that could never be answered. Then, without another word, she stood up and ran.

"Where are you going?" Tutor yelled after her. "Class isn't over. We still have to think of an answer."

Key ignored him and kept running. She ran and she ran, as fast as she could, until she reached the pond near the edge of the gorge. She could feel tears welling up in her eyes while she stepped across the lily pads and then sat in the center of her flower. As she sat there, she looked up and saw a flock of birds flying through the sky above her. She wished she were one of them. She knew birds didn't ask questions, neither did squirrels. They got to climb trees and eat nuts all day. The wolves in the woods got to run, the ducks in the pond got to swim, and the deer in the field got to play. So why, she wondered, did Tendlebees have to question an answer all day?

"It's not fair," she said. "Why can't I be like the rest of the animals?" Key wanted her wings back, but she realized that trying to answer a question that could never be answered was keeping her from doing anything else—so was thinking about the past—so was thinking about the future. She spent so much time thinking thoughts that she wasn't living. After she thought that, another thought came. And, after she thought it, she was never the same: "*If thoughts can trap me inside of my head, then what if the answer is outside instead? We used to live like a fish or a bird, but forgot how to live when we first found that word. Life's meant to be lived; instead, we just think. We're all lost in thought… that must be the link.*"

Suddenly, her eyes widened.

Her heart quickened.

Was that the answer?

Was the answer *to live?*

"It must be," she thought, because when she thought it, all the other thoughts went away. As they did, she could see the shapes in the clouds again. She could hear the water as it fell into the gorge. She could smell the flowers that grew all around her. The world was a beautiful place, and the more she looked, the more beautiful it became. As the peace of the moment spread through her head, there was only one thought that remained: *"How long has it been since I've whistled?"* She couldn't remember, but she knew it was before Tutor had taught her how to think. Then, as her past and future faded away, and with her mind as clear as a sunny day, she stood up tall, took in a deep breath, and began to whistle.

The whistle started off soft, but soon it grew so loud that it could be heard all the way across the gorge. Key giggled and kept whistling until the moon came out and the stars shown bright in the sky. Then, filled with peace, she fell asleep on her flower, which closed around her like a soft, warm cocoon. As she slept, her back began to tingle. It was the same tingling feeling she had felt just before Tutor had found her sitting in that tree. As the tingling increased, a light began to glow inside the flower and soon became as bright as a star. It glistened and sparkled as she lay in her dreams, and by that next morning, she had grown both her wings.

Key woke to the sound of birds singing in the tree above her. As she opened her eyes, she was surprised to find that she was hovering above the pond, and it took her a moment to realize what was happening.

"It can't be," she thought, and then she looked down at her reflection in the pond. There, on her back, was a pair of beautiful, white wings. She squealed, turned her head, and there they were,

just like in the pond… wings! She tried to look closer, but she kept turning in circles. So, she stopped and carefully lowered herself to the ground. As she steadied herself, she reached behind her and touched them.

They were real.

She had wings.

Overjoyed with excitement, she whistled and laughed, and lifted herself back into the sky. She flew higher and higher until she could see farther than she had ever thought she could see. She whistled again and looped through the air. Then she flew through the trees and flew past the springs to show all the others her beautiful wings.

Blink, Yep, and Twig were busy talking with Tutor about giant noses and giant eggs when Key flew down through the flowers and hovered in front of them. At first they just stared at her; then Blink gasped, Yep squealed, and Twig hooted. Tutor didn't make a sound. Instead, he fell off his toadstool and passed out on the ground. Once everyone quit gasping, squealing, and hooting, and after they revived Tutor, Key told them that she had found the answer to the question. Before she could say another word, Tutor began dancing on top of his toadstool.

"Hip-hooray!" he yelled. "She's found the answer!" He danced a little more, and then he looked down at Key, his eyes bright with excitement. "What is it?" he asked her. "What is it? What's the answer?"

"It's very simple," said Key. "It's simpler than we thought." Then she lowered herself to the ground and smiled at each of them. "The answer is—*to live*. That's why we're here, *to live*. The answer's *to live*."

Tutor stopped dancing. "But that's not an answer," he said. "It leaves too many questions. Why are we living? How did we come to be living? Where do we go when we're not living? Your answer answers none of that."

"That's because life is not about answering those questions," said Key. "Life is meant to be lived. Don't you see? We think so much about what has been, or what could be, that we forget about the present. *To live*, Tutor. The answer is *to live!*"

Tutor and the rest of the class stared at her, as if not knowing what to say. Then Twig surprised everyone when he raised his hand in the air.

"What is it, Twig?" asked Key.

Twig lowered his hand, looked around shyly, and then said, "Umm... ever since I tried to answer this question I haven't been swimming. I miss swimming."

"Then you should be swimming," said Key.

"And I miss dancing," said Yep.

"Then you should be dancing," said Key.

"And I miss climbing," said Blink.

"Then you should be climbing," said Key. "If you swam, and danced, and climbed instead of spending all day thinking, then you might get your wings."

The class was silent for a moment until Tutor raised his hand. "I miss skipping," he said. "Before I was taught the question, I used to skip all day." Then he looked at Key. "Do you think ... if I skipped again ... then I might get my wings too?"

"It's worth a try," she said. "Isn't it?"

It was worth a try, and try they did. For the rest of the day they danced, swam, skipped, and climbed. They whistled, and hooted, and laughed until they each fell asleep while wrapped in the petals of a flower. When the sun rose and lit up the sky, each of them found they had wings and could fly.

Overjoyed with excitement, Blink, Yep, Twig, and Tutor flew as fast and as far as they could before finally having to rest. They stopped in a patch of dandelions. As Key landed, they each thanked her for finding the answer.

"I could have sworn we were part of a giant egg," said Tutor. "I believed it to my core."

"We may still be," said Key.

"That's right," said Blink. "Who knows what we're part of."

"We could be part of anything," said Yep.

"...or everything," added Key.

"One big 'something,'" said Twig, who then hooted and flew toward the sky.

Tutor smiled and said, "I've spent my whole life looking for an answer." Then he paused and looked up at Twig, who was making circles in the sky. He shook his head and said, "I think I'll spend the rest of it living instead." Then he whistled and flew up to join Twig.

Key, Blink, and Yep let out a whistle as well and then flew up to join them. They rose and they dove as each of them flew. They glided, and zigzagged, and circled some too. Then they flew home through the meadows and trees to show what they'd learned to the Tendelbees.

Up on the edge of a gorge vast and deep,
Too steep to climb and too far to leap,
Key and her friends found an answer to give
And told everyone that the answer's *to live*.

Everyone tried it; they danced, swam, and climbed.
They lived in the moment with peace in their mind.
And inside a flower they each fell asleep,
Dreaming their dreams as they slept hard and deep.
As each of their flowers started to glow,

Their beautiful wings started to grow.
When they awoke, they found they could fly.
They hooted, and giggled, and took to the sky.
They looped, and swooped, and whistled some too.
Their mind became clear, and their world became new.
They quieted their disquiet and eased their unease.
There was finally an answer for the Tendlebees.

Then came the day when Key had a thought.
She wondered from where that *word* had been brought.
She crossed the great gorge to see what was there
And saw some new sights as she flew through the air.
She passed some pink trees and new flowers too.
It kept getting stranger the further she flew.
Then she found something while passing a glen,
The nest of a giant, or large creature's den.
What to do next, she couldn't decide.
Maybe she should see what might be inside.
The doorway was covered by vines with orange leaves
And bright yellow blossoms that made poor Key sneeze.
Her sneeze was so strong that it blew away dust,
Revealing a word that lay under the crust.
Carved in a stone, it reflected the sun,
And Key read each letter out one by one:
"S," "C," "H," "O," "O," "L."
But what the word meant, she just couldn't tell.
She wondered who wrote it, some creatures she guessed.
Had words led to thinking that left them all stressed,
Or had they thought thoughts but left time to play,
Creating a balance through each night and day?
Had words led to thinking that filled them with dread
Or something more loving and peaceful instead?
Had they asked "why" with no answer to give
Or found that the answer to life was *to live?*
Deciding to leave, she headed back home,
Thinking that some things were best left alone.

When she got back, it was just about night.
The stars soon came out, and the moon shown down bright.
Tired from her journey, she lay on the ground,
On top of some oak leaves, and slept safe and sound.
She lived each day after both peaceful and free.
It was a great life for a Tendlebee.

WISH WE COULD STAY

Well, little monkey, I wish we could stay.
Bombast and his bookshelf are leaving the bay.
He enjoyed the visit. Pix enjoyed it too,
And both want to see you when next they pass through.
They hope you remember as you go to bed,
Thoughts are just thoughts, and they're just in your head.
The past and the future must be put away,
For you to take in all that happens today,
Like clouds taking shape as they each pass you by,
A breathtaking sunset that colors the sky,
The soft sounds of rain, the feeling of wind,
And stars in the sky when the day's at an end.
We often forget what is out there to find,
Spending the day with the thoughts in our mind.
There's beauty, and kindness, and things you'll adore.
The world is a wondrous place to explore—
The trip of a lifetime for both you and I.
But now, my dear monkey, we must say goodbye.
And while I now leave you back up in your tree,
I'll be back soon with another story.

ABOUT THE AUTHOR

STEVE MICHAEL REEDY, MA, LPC, received his undergraduate degree in theatre, film, and television at UCLA. He later received a master's degree in counseling, and works as a licensed counselor in Dallas, Texas. He also holds licenses in varying forms of body work and teaches classes in Reiki, yoga, and meditation.

ABOUT THE ILLUSTRATOR

TOM FEE received his BFA in advertising design at the University of North Texas. Afterward, he became an art director, designer, and creative director for several small design studios. He subsequently opened Tom Fee Graphic Design where he continues his work as an illustrator.

THE FRIENDLIES' SONG

"I'm so happy, la le le.
Happy, happy, in my tree.
Join me for a cup of tea.
Happy, sappy, flappy, wee.

I'm so happy, tra la la.
Happy, happy, hip hurrah.
Join me for a bowl of slaw.
Happy, scrappy, nappy, gnaw.

I'm so happy, dip de doe.
Happy, happy, as I go.
Join me for some sugar dough.
Happy, thrappy, pappy, pough.

I'm so happy, la de do.
Happy, happy, through and through.
Join me for a nut or two.
Happy, wacky, lacky, goo."

(*ad nauseam*)

"The reason I took these to paper and pen
Is, if I should find myself back here again,
Whoever I am,
Wherever I'll be,
I hope that a monkey will read these to me."

CPSIA information can be obtained
at www.ICGtesting.com
Printed in the USA
BVHW040317110220
571996BV00004BA/6